I0545394

London

The Adlers

By

Avery Gale

LONDON
Copyright © 2019 by Avery Gale
ISBN: 978-1-944472-75-7
Print Edition

ALL RIGHTS RESERVED: This literary work may not be reproduced or transmitted in any form or by any means, including electronic or photographic reproduction, in whole or in part, without express written permission.

All characters and events in this book are fictitious. Any resemblance to actual persons living or dead is strictly coincidental.

PUBLISHER
Avery Gale
averygale.com

Cover Design by Jess Buffett at Sinfully Sweet Designs
Editing by Sandy Ebel at Personal Touch Editing
Proofreading and Second Edits by Karen Bailey

The Adlers

The siblings. Their occupations and ages at the beginning of the series:

Austin – 31 – CEO of the family oil conglomerate based in Austin, TX.

Asia – 30 – Ruthless legal eagle for the family business.

Bronx – 29 – Owns a string of car dealerships in partnership with brother, Cleveland.

Cleveland – 28 – Race car driver.

Brooklyn – 27 – Retrieval expert for big insurance companies. Semi-retired. Security consultant.

Catalina – Freelance intelligent agent, working with the CIA, MI6, Mossad, and others. Travels the world as a successful jewelry designer.

Israel – Security expert and tracker.

Kensington – Actor.

London – Chemist/Researcher.

Paris – College student.

Watch this page for updates in subsequent books in this series.

Chapter One

D R. EVAN MONROE leaned back in the black leather chair, his arms crossed over his chest as he tried to keep from rolling his eyes at the man standing at the other end of the conference room table, spewing PCBS like it was his damned job. *Hell, maybe it's a bigger part of his job than I thought.* His brother, Elijah, could take three facts and turn a five-minute discussion into an hour-long dissertation, so heavily laden with politically correct bullshit, it was a miracle anything was ever accomplished during board meetings. Evan had already been stuck here over an hour, and there was very little he loathed more than listening to someone drone on during meetings.

As a surgeon, Evan had spent the past several years working his ass off—his reputation for getting things done was well known. His medical practice had grown to the point, he needed to hire additional staff or resign himself to working twenty-four-seven. Attending one of his big brother's lectures was nowhere on his list of pleasant ways to spend the few free minutes he'd eked out of his busy work day.

Sighing to himself, Evan had to admit his frustration wasn't all due to Eli's soapbox performance. No, his foul mood had more to do with the fact the only woman who'd caught his interest in years hadn't returned his calls in the two months since he'd treated her sister. Two damned months without a word, so it seemed unlikely he was ever going to see her again. Evidently, their attraction wasn't as mutual as he'd thought it was.

Hell, maybe he should give up trying to connect with London and spend more time with his family. His dads and mom were always begging him to visit, and he knew he should take a more active role in the charitable causes the family worked so hard to support—but knowing he should and *wanting to* were turning out to be entirely different things. It didn't matter there were fewer than a handful of families like his anywhere in the world, they were still *family,* and that meant they were often as annoying as they were unique. As if the Universe had tuned in to his frustration and decided to shatter his boredom, Evan's phone vibrated in his pocket.

Seeing London's name illuminated on the screen made his heart skip a beat. Taking several steps toward the door, he swiped his finger over the screen and was shocked to see her panicked face staring back at him. The crack of gunfire and shattering glass was loud enough to draw the attention of every person in the room. Sprinting the last several feet to the door, Evan was running down the hall as he listened to London's frantic whispers. Racing to the exit, Evan hit the door so hard, it crashed against the wall as he sprinted to his truck.

"Evan, I need your help. I'm trapped in the small lab at Gates." He knew the facility she was talking about, but he hadn't known she was so fucking close. "I'm going to sneak out the back and make a dash for the woods." It wasn't necessary for London to tell him to pick her up, he was already starting his truck. He was only minutes from her, but he knew it was going to feel like hours of travel time.

Evan watched London's ashen face turn frantically from one side to the other, confusion layering on her already frightened expression. "B was here. I don't know how. I don't know where she went." As he put the truck in gear, the diesel motor roared as he sped out of the parking lot. Evan saw her moving out of the dimly lit lab into the black night, and he hoped like hell the facility's perimeter lighting wouldn't give away her location.

"I'll find you, London. As soon as we disconnect, I want you to make sure the GPS on your phone is shut off." With his heightened night vision and a keen sense of smell, he could find her with his eyes closed. "Shut the phone down before you run, baby." He'd used the endearment without thinking and was grateful she didn't seem alarmed by the overly familiar term. Dividing his attention between the road and his phone was a dangerous game. Evan knew he needed to disconnect and focus on driving.

"Now, London! Go!" The fear he saw flash in her eyes before the screen went blank was like a punch to his gut.

The pale, shaken woman he'd just spoken to was nothing like the confident chemist he'd first met over a year ago at a medical conference. Before attending the annual event, Evan had read several of her published papers and looked forward to meeting her. The moment their gazes met, all his questions evaporated into slender tendrils of white smoke he would have sworn danced between them like something out of a damned cartoon.

London Adler had enchanted him. She'd zeroed in on him from the stage, and that moment was the only time she'd stumbled over her words during the entire two hours she'd been up there.

Her presentation included an intense question-and-answer session where she'd been grilled about the rumors she was working on a project expected to change the entire landscape of cancer treatment and vaccinations, but she'd deftly dodged all the inquiries. Evan had worried the rumors alone would paint a huge target on her, and hearing she'd been attacked in a lab sent a chill of foreboding up Evan's spine. Activating the communication system in his truck, he instructed the computer to text Luke Grayson. Grayson and London's sister, Brooklyn, were currently living in New Mexico, busy planning their upcoming wedding.

Is Brooklyn with you? Evan was relieved when the other man responded immediately.

Yes. Why? What's going on? There was a sense of urgency in Luke's response Evan hadn't expected, making him wonder what was happening on the other end.

Not sure. Will update ASAP. Disconnecting the system, he sent out a telepathic call to the pack's security team, asking them to watch the perimeter since it bordered the Gates' property. Once he'd received assurance they were already in place, he could fully concentrate on the road and getting to London as quickly as possible.

Sliding around the last turn into the wooded area butting up against the rear of the Gates research facility, Evan extinguished the lights of his truck. His night vision made the headlights unnecessary, and they would only serve to herald his arrival. Shooters wouldn't expect him to be able to see them, and he hoped like hell it would even the playing field enough he could get London the hell out of here. Rolling to a stop, he was out of the truck and running between the thick trunks of trees before it finished rocking from the force. He sprinted toward a figure he spotted crouched behind a small outcropping of rocks, sending up a silent prayer to the Universe he'd found her in time.

LONDON HUDDLED AGAINST the rough bark of the largest tree she'd been able to find in her mad dash for cover. Crouched low with her arms wrapped tightly around her knees, she focused on making herself as small as possible. She hadn't seen or heard any sign of whoever had blindsided her in the lab, but that didn't mean they weren't out there—waiting.

Why hadn't she called her brothers when the emails started? Damn it all to hell, she should have at least talked to Luke. Luke Grayson, her future brother-in-law, was a top-tier computer security expert whose connections were second to none... and God only knew how frustrated he was going to be she hadn't asked for help. It was going to be a toss-up who would be the most annoyed... Austin, Israel, or Luke.

At first, she'd thought the emails were nothing more than the run-of-the-mill nonsense all medical researchers deal with—people who either believe a scientist was stonewalling progress that had the potential to save lives, or they were convinced a scientist was trying to play God.

Since rumors began circulating about her work a year and a half ago, she'd dealt with people at both ends of the spectrum without incident, but this time, things had escalated quickly when she ignored the communication.

In the beginning, she suspected the man she'd dated briefly last year was responsible, simply because there had been something vaguely familiar about the tone of the communication. She still wasn't convinced he wasn't involved, but she couldn't prove he was either. *I should have known he wasn't interested in me. Hot, rich guys don't give two twits about lab-rats.*

Once she'd learned who he worked for, London had confronted him with the information she'd received anonymously. The Interpol report had been remarkably informative, detailing Franklin Cordesi's connection to a large group of pharmaceutical companies known as the Consortium. The documentation included an outline of his current assignment—gaining the trust and compliance of chemist London Adler. He'd tried to explain, but she hadn't been interested in his excuses. London had been disappointed but resolute. She'd blocked his number and email without a moment's hesitation.

London was still mortified at how easily she'd been taken in. While it was true she didn't have much... okay, make that *any* experience dating, she was usually a better judge of character. The embarrassing fiasco had shaken her confidence to the point, she hadn't had the courage to return Evan's calls when he expressed an interest in her and began calling after he'd treated Brooklyn a couple months ago. *But who was the first person you called when you were being shot at? Evan. So maybe on some instinctual level, you trust him…* hell, her mind was spinning so fast it was probably going to turn to mush. *And you really need to stop talking to yourself as well.*

The roar of a distant motor had her sucking in a quick breath. She sent up a silent prayer to the Universe it was Evan racing to her rescue and not back-up called by the lunatic inside. How had the shooter known she was there? After all, her car was hiding in plain sight in the small neighboring town. Maybe he'd been as surprised by her presence as she was by his? And holy freaking Annie Oakley, how professional could he be? She wasn't a firearms expert, but it seemed like he was a damned poor shot if you asked her. Now that she thought about it, it was almost as if he'd been trying to miss her.

Damn it, after she'd started receiving those damned emails a few weeks ago, she had deliberately varied her work schedule to the point, there were a few times she'd wondered if she wasn't going to meet herself at the door. She'd worked such long hours, it had often been a surprise to walk out of the lab and discover it was already dawn. Several times, she'd woken up with her head resting on folded arms atop her desk without a clue if it was daylight or dark.

Pulling her arms tighter around her legs, London cursed not having a jacket to ward off the chilly night air. The lab coat she still wore—all but shredded by falling glass from the windows being shot out as she'd been hiding behind her desk—offered little protection from the low temperature and stiff breeze. Falling glass raining down on her had poked holes in her damned scalp and shoulders too. The facility director, a greasy-haired man who reminded London of a weasel, had assured her the windows of her lab would withstand anything short of a major terrorist attack. *Yeah, we're going to have a nice long chat about that... if I manage to survive.*

When she'd first leased the lab, she'd made it clear safety was her number one concern, even asking her brother, Israel, to do a walkthrough to make recommendations. She could live with the older equipment, drab paint, and dingy floors, but she'd asked endless questions about the facility's security. The foundation's board of directors had even agreed to add several features Israel recommended. Having nine siblings was often a pain in the ass, but as a security specialist, Israel's insight had been a blessing. *I just wish he was here now.*

Burying her face deeper in her folded arms, hoping her pale face wouldn't act as a beacon broadcasting her location, she silently cursed the gaunt woman who'd looked back at her from the mirror this morning. Damn, she needed to get outside more. Looking at her reflection in the mirror, after her usual three hours of sleep, she'd gasped at the pale-faced figure staring back at her. Hell, she looked like she was auditioning for a part in a damned vampire movie. Haunted, red-rimmed eyes with deep purple half-moons shadowing them made her look more like Uncle Fester's long-lost daughter than a twenty-three-year-old woman.

London knew she'd been burning the candle at both ends, but there was no question the damned clock was running out. She was convinced it was only a matter of time before the group trying to recruit her gave up and decided to steal her research instead. London wasn't stupid.

Nor was she naïve. When push came to shove, the billions of dollars at stake made her an insignificant point of collateral damage.

The snap of a nearby twig yanked her back to the moment, and she fought hard to not raise her face. With a little luck, maybe her long hair would conceal enough of her white lab coat to make her blend into her surroundings. *Oh yeah, those blonde curls are going to be great camouflage.* Hearing her name whispered on the soft breeze, London strained to recognize the voice.

Holding her breath, she willed herself to stay focused and fight the urge to flee. She wasn't sure how long she'd been exposed to the cold and curled into a tight ball, but she was sure her legs were going to be too stiff to run when she first stood up. Who are you kidding, London? *You have been locked in a lab for months, you couldn't run down the hall to the water fountain. Jesus, Joseph, and Mary, I'm talking to myself again.*

Strong arms encircled her, and adrenaline hurtled through her system faster than she'd ever imagined possible. London's body exploded into action, but her stiff muscles prevented her from getting to her feet. Stiffening, she raised her face, but before she could suck in a deep breath to scream, a warm hand covered her mouth.

"Shhh, baby, it's Evan." She'd been a half a heartbeat from sinking her teeth into his palm when her mind registered who was holding her. London knew her eyes had to be the size of saucers, but she wasn't sure he'd see them in the dark... her brothers were another story. They could see in the pitch blackness as easily as in broad daylight—just one of the traits they'd inherited from their father. She'd always envied their gifts and wondered why she'd gotten left out of the genetic lottery.

"I'm going to remove my hand but only if you promise to not scream. I can tell by your frightened expression you are dangerously close to shock."

What? How the hell can he see my expression? Think, London. You can figure this out. Her mind was so scattered, nothing was making any sense, her thoughts pinging around like the damned steel balls in her brother, Kensington's pinball machine.

It had been obvious Austin respected Evan when the two of them huddled in the hallway during Brooklyn's stay at the clinic. *And you know Austin doesn't like anyone who isn't like him in one way or another.* She'd suspected both men were sexual Dominants, but she wasn't sure. *Maybe it's not the Dom-thing?* She tried to force her brain into gear, but the damned thing wasn't working right. Why couldn't she make her thoughts follow some sort of logical progression? *It's probably as frozen as the rest of you, and if you don't stop talking to yourself, someone's going to drop a net over your crazy self.*

"We need to get out of here as quickly as possible. I have back-up guarding the perimeter, but I'd rather not draw any more attention than necessary." When she started to turn her head, his large hands framed the sides of her face, and she sensed more than saw his frown. She was struggling to stay calm, but the threads of her control were being stretched dangerously thin.

"How did you find me so quickly? It's so dark and—" He cut her off, pressing a finger against her lips.

"Let's go. There will be plenty of time for explanations

once you're safe." He stood, holding out his hand for her to follow suit, but her cold muscles wouldn't cooperate. The more she struggled, the closer she was to toppling over like some damned Weeble. Without missing a beat, he scooped her into his arms and began walking. She marveled at how effortlessly he navigated through the densely wooded area, easily stepping side to side around obstacles while she could barely make out his features mere inches from her face. As the second burst of adrenaline she'd experienced in less than hour quickly faded, London felt herself wilting against Evan's muscular chest.

Tucking her face into the side of his neck, she breathed in the fresh smell of soap and something wild she couldn't identify, but it was the underlying scent that caught her attention. She'd smelled it somewhere before, but her mind was reeling from everything she'd been through the past few weeks, and nothing was making any sense. In the back of her mind, she connected the outdoor scent to her father when he'd return from one of his midnight runs. Exhaustion and frustration washed over her as she tried to remember the details. What good was being considered one of the best and brightest in her field if she couldn't fit together the simplest puzzle pieces of her own life? Finally succumbing to the adrenaline crash, London let her eyes drift closed, allowing the darkness to pull her under.

Chapter Two

E VAN KNEW THE moment London let go. She had to
have been running on fumes because she hadn't put
forth any protest when he'd picked her up—not that the
petite beauty had much choice since it had been painfully
obvious she couldn't even stand. There wasn't a chance in
hell she could have walked out under her own steam. His
enhanced senses helped him spot her from the truck, so it
had only taken him a few seconds to reach her side.
Parking close had seemed like an advantage, but now he
regretted not being able to keep her cradled in his arms for
more than a few heartbeats.

Approaching the spot where she'd been hiding, Evan
had called her name in soft whispers he hoped wouldn't
carry too far on the breeze. He'd picked up a twig and
snapped it to warn her he was nearby. Her nearly silent
gasp let him know the shivering, huddled woman he could
see so clearly had finally heard him, but she didn't move a
muscle. Evan might not be as strong an empath as his new
friend, Luke, but as a shifter, the smell of fear had overwhelmed him as soon as he'd stepped outside his truck. As
a physician, Evan damn well recognized an adrenaline
crash when he saw one, and the petite bundle in his arms

had just gone head-first into the wall.

The drive to his clinic was short since the facility was nearby on the edge of pack land. A hundred years ago, a sharp decline in pack numbers forced several groups to band together. Pooling their vast financial resources, they'd been able to put together a large parcel of land between Boston and New York City, enabling members to easily commute either direction for outside career opportunities. Even though many of their members worked for businesses owned by the group or individual members, many others worked in what they referred to as the non-shifter world.

The security at Evan's clinic was second to none. Most people assumed he'd implemented all safety features to protect the privacy of his high-profile patients, but that was only a small part of the reason. He also treated shifters since their medical care couldn't be trusted to anyone outside their community. The unique nature of their bodies and the rampant rumor mills of most traditional medical facilities *always* spelled disaster for shifters the world over.

A few months earlier, when Jace Garrett called asking for Evan's help, he'd been tempted to send one of his staff. Luke Grayson, a fellow Club Isola member, had received information Brooklyn Adler had put herself in a precarious situation. It was highly likely she could be hurt, and the group going after her hadn't wanted to take any chances.

Jace and the rest of the team coordinating her rescue made a lifesaving call for several reasons. Brooklyn had grossly overestimated her ability to overcome the exhaustion leveling her, and she'd underestimated the luck of the security team who'd followed her out of the large estate she'd broken into. After being shot on a small private island off the coast while retrieving a stolen artifact, Brooklyn Adler landed dead-center on Emilio Mendoza's hit list. Mendoza was not only a criminal of the first order, he was also as crazy as they came and currently, in Federal custody where he would likely spend the rest of his life.

As a long-time member of Club Isola, Evan wasn't about to turn his back on Jace or club owner, Ian McGregor. Hell, the thought of denying their request had never occurred to him—the only question had been which members of his staff to call in to assist once they'd moved her to the clinic. Since Brooklyn's injuries hadn't been life-threatening, he'd worked with a skeleton crew, but that hadn't kept her brothers from noticing they were among shifters.

Austin Adler's position of leadership in his own large pack would have been reason enough for Evan to step up to help, but it was Brooklyn's relationship to London that had been his real impetus. The woman currently curled against his chest—trembling from the bone-deep chill she'd gotten when forced to flee into the cold night air without a damned jacket—had been the real reason Evan hadn't sent one of his proteges.

Setting her inside his truck, he reached over her to fasten her seatbelt and watched as London's eyes fluttered open. The stark fear he saw reflected in their depths was like a knife to his heart. Pulling her into his arms, he kissed the top of her head and simply held her for several long seconds—seconds he worried they didn't have to spare. In those few moments, he'd felt her trust, and it was a gift he would always treasure.

Evan didn't need the truck's headlights as he drove slowly back out of the woods, so he kept them off in hopes the black pickup wouldn't be an easy target. He planned to use a little-known trail, bringing them out closer to the clinic's secured back entrance, it would be foolish to draw any unnecessary attention. No need to alert anyone looking for London that she'd had help escaping. The more time the shooter spent looking for her was more time they had to figure out what the hell was going on. And he damned well didn't want to advertise the secondary entrance into the clinic's secured perimeter. If anyone had seen him enter the wooded area, they'd expect him to leave by the same route, meaning they'd be waiting near the entrance to follow.

He'd only driven a short distance when he heard the latch on London's safety belt release. Glancing to his right, he met her gaze and saw understanding in her eyes. He wasn't surprised she'd pulled together pieces of information and knew how he was easily navigating in the pitch dark. Turning his attention back to the road, Evan waited for her rejection. With a soft sigh, she scooted closer before laying down. With her cheek pressed against his thigh, her warm breath moved through his cotton shirt, washing over his abdomen making his cock sit up and take notice. Twitching a fraction of an inch from her face, his dick didn't give a rat's ass she'd been traumatized—the selfish bastard was thickening and preparing to play. Christ, he was going to be rock hard in a New York minute if he didn't get control over his rampant libido.

As a Dom, control was a point of pride, but there was

something about London Adler that seemed to shatter his control. Her scent haunted him, his soul recognized hers, and holding himself back was getting more and more difficult every time they were together. When she splayed her small hand over his chest, the cool tips of her fingers pushed between the buttons of his shirt until they were pressed against his bare chest. Evan could feel the longing for human connection coming off her in waves, making it damned hard to keep from pulling over and setting her on his lap. Laying his own hand over hers, he slid his fingers tight atop hers and pressed her palm firmly against his heart.

"I've got you, sweetheart. Close your eyes and just breathe. Let me take care of you, and we'll be out of here before you know it." With the press of a button on the steering wheel, Evan activated his phone and put in a call to the clinic's security office. "I'll be coming up to the back gate in three minutes. I want it open and waiting. No one else comes or goes without my prior approval, and that includes employees."

"Yes, sir. I will activate the gate in two minutes so you won't need to slow down. I'm already tracking your vehicle." The man who'd answered was new to the security department, but Evan had known the man all of his life. Seth Keller's father, Abe, was the clinic's chief of security, so the younger man had practically grown up in the control room.

"Call your dad and give him a heads up. I want all security beefed up until further notice. As soon as he's onsite, get someone to cover your post and find me." He disconnected the call without waiting for Seth's response. Driving through the open gate, he checked his rearview mirror, breathing a sigh of relief when he saw the steel reinforced panels were already sliding back into position. Rounding the corner of the main clinic, Evan smiled when he saw Seth had already opened the door to his private garage.

When he'd first envisioned the clinic, Evan had wanted a much smaller compound, including a scaled-down version of the private residence he currently occupied. The pack's elderly architect argued his concept was inadequate and scolded him for not having enough faith in his future. Evan hadn't been easily swayed; he'd opposed the added expense, not wanting any unnecessary financial burden, but in the end, he'd relented. Every year on the anniversary of the clinic's opening, he took architect John Whiteside to dinner and thanked him for his insight. To the casual observer, his home appeared to be separated from the clinic by a beautifully landscaped courtyard, but the two buildings were connected by two separate underground tunnels. There was a third tunnel leading directly to the main house where Eli now lived.

London's brother, Austin had complimented him on his attention to security details. Evan had laughed to himself, wondering how impressed Austin would be if he knew the truth of the situation. Evan's pack was tireless in their dedication to keeping their members safe from discovery. The dangers of being exposed as a shifter were enormous and far-reaching. History had proven how risky it was for non-shifters to learn the truth about their neighbors—guarding their secrets was literally a life or death issue.

The southern packs didn't live in as tightly knit communities as their counterparts in the northeastern United States, a fact Evan had always found fascinating. He had several theories, but he'd never had the chance to talk to one of their leaders about the difference. If things worked out with London in the way Evan hoped, he and Eli would have plenty of opportunities to speak to Austin Adler. Smiling to himself as he parked, he looked at the woman beginning to stir beside him.

"Come on, sweetheart, let's get you inside. I want to look at those cuts and make sure we get them cleaned properly." His words were met by London's glazed expression, telling him she still wasn't fully recovered from her exposure to low temperatures and the shock of being attacked in her lab. Helping her from the truck, he noticed she was clutching something in her left hand. "What is that, London?"

She didn't respond immediately, causing him to pause his steps and turn to her in question. When she slowly opened her hand, revealing several high-capacity flash drives, he couldn't hold back his smile.

"Your research?" When she nodded, he chuckled. "Good girl." Comprehending the full meaning, he framed her pale face with his hands and asked, "You knew you were in danger, didn't you?" When her eyes went glassy with unshed tears, Evan sighed—damn he was a sucker for tears, and hers would likely shred his heart.

"Come on baby, we have a lot to talk about before the cavalry arrives." As if he'd summoned the intrusion, the speaker system above them snapped as it clicked on, causing London to jump as he led her toward the door. Seth's voice announced the impending arrival of the security chief and several other *community members,* and Evan smiled at the younger man's use of the code for the pack. Giving permission for them to enter, Evan waited because he'd noticed the speaker hadn't clicked off. Tightening his hold on London's elbow when she would have taken another step to the door, he quietly waited.

"Sorry if I startled you, Dr. Adler." Seth's quiet apology would confirm what London would have no doubt already suspected if she wasn't already so distracted. There were security cameras monitoring the garage.

Leaning close, Evan whispered, "There are only cameras in the garage. Once we step into the house, we'll have complete privacy unless we activate the system. I'll fill you in on the details once we've gotten you settled." Thanking Seth, they moved on once he knew the other man had nothing to add. Evan smiled at her soft gasp of surprise when they stepped through the door into what he jokingly referred to as a mud-room. The enormous space would be more accurately described as a large recreation area with a washer and dryer than simply a place to shed soiled clothing. A heated, indoor pool surrounded by small palm trees took up the right half of the cavernous space while gym and recreation equipment occupied the left side.

"Holy shit. If this is your back door, I can hardly wait to see what the front looks like. My whole apartment would fit in your pool… with plenty of room to spare."

Evan turned to her and raised a brow in question. When her eyes finally met his, he tilted his head to the side, letting her know he was waiting for her to explain. He'd done his research and knew her parents hadn't been wealthy, but her brother had taken the small corporation all ten siblings held stock in and turned it into a multibillion-dollar conglomerate. She'd have access to enough money to live in something larger than his damned pool.

"I had a small apartment down the hall from the lab." Her softly spoken confession surprised him.

"Had?" He knew he needed to get her further inside and take a look at the cuts she'd sustained, but something about the way her eyes darted to the side when she'd answered set off warning bells.

"Well, I packed up all my stuff early this morning." She started chewing on the bottom lip, and he could practically hear her mind spinning. "Everything is in my car." She paused for long seconds as she once again scanned the room they were standing in before meeting his questioning gaze. She sagged, letting out a breath he doubted she realized she'd been holding.

"Where is your car, London?" This was going to take too long if he had to drag every piece of information from her, and the clock was ticking.

"It's parked in town… in front of the Sheriff's Office. I figured that was as safe as anyplace." Evan agreed, she'd probably chosen one of the safest places available although he wished like hell, she'd called him instead.

"What kind of car is it? I'm friends with the Sheriff, I'll make sure he secures it for you." He saw her eyes widen in surprise, but she gave him the information which he quickly passed along.

"He won't have the keys. How will he be able to secure it?"

Evan chuckled softly. For a woman whose older sister was one of the most sought-after thieves in the world, she was awfully naïve about how easily a car could be moved without the benefit of a key. Brooklyn Adler had been a retrieval expert for the world's largest insurers until her recent retirement—and retirement was a term to be used cautiously. From what Evan had heard, no one expected the pint-sized burglar to walk away cleanly from the lucrative career she'd loved more for the adrenaline rush than the money.

Hell, he wasn't even considering London's sister, Catalina. Cat Adler was a contract agent for a plethora of alphabet agencies from several countries. It was hard to imagine her theft skills were anything less than stellar. Cat's cover as a jewelry designer favored by the rich and famous around the world allowed her to travel freely in and out of areas where others would have raised flags.

Smiling down at London while her intelligent eyes once again scanned the room, taking careful stock of her surroundings, Evan was reminded how petite the next to youngest Adler was compared to his six-foot-six frame. At his height, he was well accustomed to towering over people, but London's five-foot-nothing stature made the difference between them particularly obvious.

Cradling her in his arms as he'd carried her out of the nearby woods, he'd noted how rail thin London was beneath the shredded lab coat she wore and assumed she'd been too busy working to eat—a hazard he knew all too well. If it hadn't been for a couple of non-medical roommates in college, he might well have starved to death.

London's reputation as a brilliant researcher was enviable, not only because she was so incredibly young but also because she'd managed to find previously unknown links between several illnesses and vaccinations. Of course, anytime a chemist starts looking too closely at vaccines, big pharma takes notice—and they'd damned well taken note after London's presentation last year.

Evan recently heard there were new rumors London was tracking several specific compounds she'd identified in the composition of the vaccines, oddities suspected to be related to the links because they appeared to be anomalies. He could hardly wait to ask her questions, but given her reputation for fiercely protecting her research, Evan wasn't sure she would answer. Hell, from what he'd heard, she'd cut all of her staff loose, then disappeared into a lab several weeks ago. Little had he known she was literally next door. Shaking his head, Evan realized he'd been so lost in his own thoughts, he hadn't answered her question.

"I think Trin will be able to figure it out." As understatements went, Evan's was huge. Trinity Frost's story was a classic troublemaker turns cop saga. He'd nearly driven pack leaders insane before one of the senior members of the board suggested assigning him to shadow the local Sheriff. The controversial move turned out to be a stroke of genius. Trinity's experience on the wrong side of the law gave him a unique insight and also helped him connect with other young people who were dancing over the line.

"Trin?" Evan's words must have broken through the fog in London's mind because, for the first time, he could see the fiery spark in her eyes that had first caught his attention.

"Trinity Frost is our Sheriff. I'm sure you'll get a chance to meet him—I'd be surprised if he isn't one of the

22

men headed this way now. He's intense, but he'll have your back, so level with him." The warning shouldn't be necessary, but he'd seen the effect Trinity had on people—the man could be intimidating as hell.

"Come on, let's get you cleaned up. You'll feel better meeting everyone if you don't look like a frozen wood sprite." He watched as her eyes widened in surprise. When her hands went to her hair, she gasped and nodded. The wild blonde mass of curls was filled with twigs and leaves, and he suspected she'd need a shower to work out all the tangles.

Holding out his hand, he was pleased when she only hesitated a second before placing her slender fingers in his palm. Closing his warm hand around her cold one, Evan fought the temptation to pull her into his arms. Damn it, he just wanted to hold her for a few moments. Hell, at this point, it was probably more about convincing himself she was alright rather than trying to reassure her she was safe.

Leading her further into the house, he didn't stop to show her around. There was no question the place was going to fill up quickly, and he wanted her settled before the cavalry arrived. Without giving any consideration to the implications, Evan led her past several perfectly suited guest bedrooms with en suite bathrooms before leading her into the master suite. When she hesitated at the door, he shook his head and gave her hand a quick tug. The difference in their sizes and her exhaustion meant what little resistance he'd felt faded quickly, and she followed him into a bathroom larger than most bedrooms.

"We need to get you out of those clothes, so I can assess the damage." Her eyes went wide, and for a few heartbeats, he wondered if she was going to bolt before her chin tipped up in defiance. He held back his smile at the small bit of bravado, knowing how much the move must have cost her. *She might have more luck selling it if she wasn't weaving on her feet.*

"I'll undress and wrap myself in a towel while you wait outside." Her voice was stronger than he'd expected, but he'd still heard the edge of arousal beneath the surface.

"No, sweetheart, you are already balanced precariously on the edge of collapse, and I don't want you falling in here. Your head isn't meant to bounce off the marble floor or counters. You've already had enough tonight, let's not take any unnecessary risks." Meeting her mutinous glare, he used his fingers to grip her chin, ensuring all her focus was on him. "I'm a physician, London. You do not have anything I haven't seen. Take off your damned clothes, and I'll wrap you in one of the towels from the warmer, but I am not leaving the room. Are we clear?"

He knew the power of the compelling element in his voice, and he was always careful when using it—it wasn't a tool he used indiscriminately. As a sexual Dominant, Evan only used his Dom-voice with submissives—anything else a serious ethical question when it came to the safe, sane, and consensual guiding tenant of the lifestyle. The words were more than a guide, they were the law at Club Isola. Ian McGregor's integrity and insistence on the strict adherence to every possible safety measure for his members was one of the reasons Evan felt the club was worth the travel time. There were closer clubs, but none with the same reputation as Club Isola.

Chapter Three

THE BUZZING IN London's head was getting louder, and the damned dark spots dancing in her vision seemed to be growing exponentially with every second. Damn it, she should have known better than to call the one man who made her heart beat out her chest. Why didn't she call… hell, who would she have called? Surely Austin would have known someone to call. *He'd have called Evan, and you know it, London.*

She'd seen the way Austin and Israel's nostrils had flared when the three of them had met outside Brooklyn's room. After watching her father and brothers over the years, London knew that response happened when they were meeting other shifters for the first time. It always amazed her how closely their behavior mirrored the lupine sub-species. Her family might roll their eyes at her scientific way of looking at the world, but she didn't care. Things were easier to understand if they could be classified into groups and sub-groups. She tried to write off the connection between the men as fellow Doms, but it had been more than that.

London knew their instant respect for each other had gone a long way toward explaining why Austin hadn't made any attempt to move Brooklyn to another facility. Well… that and Dr. Evan Monroe's reputation among the rich and persnickety. Hell, the man was practically revered among the elite patients who used his clinic. When she'd first gotten the call about B, London had been surprised to learn the man who'd caught her interest at a medical conference was the one treating her sister.

Standing in front of Evan now, London realized how significantly she'd underestimated her attraction to him. Nothing like jumping out of the frying pan into the flames. Damn, she was in a freaking pickle… *and why is it so damned dark in here?*

"Fucking hell."

In the dark recesses of her mind, London heard Evan's curse a split second before her knees folded out from under her. Warm arms surrounded her, but it was his lips sealing over hers that made her suck in a deep breath. The infusion of oxygen cleared her vision for a few seconds before desire exploded in her chest, making the black dots come roaring back with a vengeance.

"Breathe, London."

Breathe? Is he kidding? His kiss turned off my brain and ignited everything else—how am I supposed to remember to breathe?

He released her lips much sooner than she'd have liked, making her inhale sharply, trying to regain her equilibrium.

"Take off your clothes, sweetheart. I need to check your cuts before you get in the shower." *What? He wants to stop kissing to look at cuts? What the hell? Way to be two for two, London.* "I recognize that look, baby, and you can push any thought I don't want you right on out of your head. This isn't a rejection, it's me trying to take care of you despite the fact my cock is about to explode." *Wow. Okay. This is new.*

London had never had a man speak to her so bluntly, and she couldn't decide whether her shock came from the words themselves or her reaction to them. She'd felt a rush of liquid heat coat the pulsing folds of her sex, and her core clenched in unfulfilled need. Heat built in her core until she was forced to shift in an effort to relieve the ache. Evan smiled down at her indulgently, but she knew he wouldn't be dissuaded for long, so she nodded her understanding.

Refocusing on what she knew, rather than all the questions swirling around in her head, brought back some of the emotional balance she'd need to get through what she suspected was coming. Once she'd figured out her brothers were Dominants, she'd started reading up on the subject. Being analytical, London made it a habit to never make a judgment based on emotion, and her first response to the explanations of their take-charge, *I'm the boss of you* nonsense hadn't been pretty. Now, she understood their need for control in other areas of their lives was closely linked to their lifestyle, and while she had no plans to learn anything more about her brothers' particular kinks, finding out about Evan's was something else entirely.

London had always known her brothers were different, but it hadn't been until they hit puberty and began to shift that she'd understood the extent of those differences. None of the girls in the Adler family had made the change or appeared to possess any shifter traits, but her parents had assured them their own unique gifts would come with time and love. For her, their assurances had fallen on deaf ears—London hadn't been convinced and had said so.

Asia, Brooklyn, Catalina, and Paris had agreed but hadn't put forth the logical arguments she'd presented. London contended there was no empirical evidence to support their claim, and to their credit, they'd listened patiently without interrupting. They hadn't argued their case, they'd merely nodded their understanding, their knowing gazes moving over her in loving approval.

It had never mattered to her deeply spiritual parents that she was a scientist to the bone. They'd loved her unconditionally, despite her tendency to question everything and argue with them at every turn. Their acceptance had eventually broken through the worst of her barriers, and she'd learned to be more open to things she couldn't easily explain. No sooner had she let the possibilities of a world outside her lab take root than everything had changed. Her parents had been taken from her, and she'd felt more vulnerable than ever because the shields she'd hidden behind as a kid were no longer impermeable.

"Sweetheart, you need to come back to me. I know you can hear me, but I need you to focus for a few minutes, okay?"

Shaking her head trying to clear the fog, London looked up into Evan's eyes and wondered why she felt so warm. Running her fingers down over her torso, she was shocked to discover she was covered in an ultra-soft towel… and nothing else.

"How?" He must have understood the essence of her confusion because he grinned sheepishly.

"You're remarkably cooperative when you're crashing,

baby." She probably should be angry, but she wasn't. Hell, it was painfully obvious she hadn't been capable of removing the shredded clothing herself, so she didn't feel she had any right to complain about him helping her. And he was right, he was a doctor, and she didn't have anything he hadn't seen although hers might not be in the same condition as those of the women at Club Isola.

Oh yeah, she knew Dr. Evan Monroe was a member of one of the most exclusive kink clubs in the country. What she didn't know was why he attended one so far from his home or what his particular kinks were. That wasn't to say she wasn't curious, but her eavesdropping hadn't yielded all the answers to the questions that had raced through her mind. She'd stood silently in the hall outside his office, during the darkest hours before dawn while Brooklyn slept soundly a few doors down and listened as he'd updated Jace Garrett and Ian McGregor on Brooklyn's condition.

London had often heard the expression, six degrees of separation, but in the world of the rich and kinky, she was beginning to suspect the number was much lower. Damn it to dancing dip-sticks, she wondered if anybody had done a study on the frequency of kink among the uber-wealthy and famous. She was dangerously close to falling into what her family called her scientist coma, but strong fingers gripped her chin, drawing her attention to the concerned face of the man staring down at her.

"Sweetheart, I need you to stay with me. It's one thing to help you out of tattered clothing so I can get you wrapped in something warm without you being complete-ly cognizant, but it would be an entirely different matter to do any sort of medical exam without your permission when I know you're capable of giving it." When she nodded, he shook his head. "Words, London. You have to say the words. We'll begin as we intend to go." Her breath caught—she'd read those words in her research and knew what he was saying. Feeling her cheeks heat, she wondered if he could feel the electricity arcing between them.

"Yes. I want you to make sure everything is okay because I'd really like to get in that shower." Holy hell, the man's shower was enormous, and the overhead rain showerheads would go a long way to help detangle her hair. He'd already started the water, and she could hear the sound of falling water along the back wall and wondered if there was a waterfall or another group of heads she couldn't see.

He didn't answer, but his quick grin as he followed her gaze told her he'd seen the longing in her eyes. Running his fingers over her scalp, he separated sections of her thick hair several times to check an injury he'd felt or in reaction to her flinch.

"There are several small lacerations, but I don't think you'll require stitches."

She was relieved, knowing there was at least one battle she didn't have to fight. London wouldn't have let him shave spots on her head without waging an epic battle. She might not be fully back in the game, but she wasn't letting him or anyone else near her hair with shears.

"You know, sweetheart, I've seen that look before, and I know what you're thinking. I wouldn't shave a hair on your lovely head unless it was a big damned cut." She could hear the amused tone in his voice and relaxed.

"Sorry. It's just that I remember all the times my

brothers came home from the emergency room with bald patches because they'd done something stupid and ended up cracking open their skulls." She took a deep breath and chuckled. "Honestly, it's a wonder they don't all sit around drooling and staring blankly out the window. I'm sure the insurance company had to roll their eyes every time our family was mentioned." Now that her body was settling down, London found herself studying Evan as he looked over the numerous nicks and scratches covering her arms.

He was even better looking up close than she remembered, and that was saying a lot. The first time she'd seen him, he'd shaken her to her core. Her eyes met his from the stage, and her entire body felt as though it had been infused with heat. The intensity of her reaction had been almost frightening, and it sent her usual unflappable public persona reeling. On stage, Dr. London Adler was confident and poised. In person, she often found herself lacking on both fronts. She'd be loathed to admit the difference, but that didn't change the truth.

He finished his cursory examination frowning at a deep puncture on her shoulder. "When was your last tetanus vaccination?" When she didn't answer, Evan frowned. "Longer than a year?"

"Yes. I think I had one when I was sixteen although it might have been earlier."

"Sixteen? Jesus."

She wanted to laugh at the look of frustration on his face but decided it wasn't in her best interest since she wasn't exactly on her home turf. *Who are you kidding? You don't have any home turf. All your stuff is in your damned car.*

"I'll call the clinic and have someone bring one over, I

don't want to wait until tomorrow since I have no idea what was going on in that damned lab." She knew he was right, but just the thought of getting a shot scared the hell out of her, and London felt her whole body stiffen in response. Evan's attention zeroed in on her response and shook his head. "You have got to be kidding me. You're one of the most gifted medical research chemists in the country—hell, probably the world, and you're scared of a needle?"

"Who said I'm scared?" She wasn't sure her false bravado was believable, but as the ninth in a family of ten kids, she learned a long time ago it was always best to fake it until you can make it.

"Baby, I can smell your fear. You know the body's chemistry changes with apprehension, and it's coming off you in waves."

She sucked in a quick breath because he was not only right, it was the second time he'd given her a hint to his special abilities.

EVAN SAW A flash of recognition in London's eyes a split second before she looked away. By the time he used his fingers to bring her chin back up, she'd masked the emotions in what he had suspected was a well-practiced move. He was going to enjoy teaching the sweet little chemist how to let go and embrace the passion he knew simmered beneath the surface. The longing he'd seen in London's eyes as she'd watched Luke Grayson with her sister, Brooklyn, had told him how much she ached for the same acceptance. Luke and Brooklyn had been close friends for years, but the little spitfire burglar had only recently allowed their relationship to move to the next level. While London had been watching them, he'd studied her.

What he'd seen had surprised him. There was a void in London's life. The brilliant woman behind some of the most significant research currently taking place in the medical field was unfulfilled and lonely. Evan wondered if she realized she was a submissive. There wasn't a Dom worth his salt who wouldn't recognize the need dancing in her sparkling blue eyes. He doubted she would ever be the kind of sub who could walk into a club and scene with any Dom who approached her—it would take a very special Dom to claim London Adler's heart.

"Let's worry about the vaccination later, baby. Right now, it's more important to get you cleaned up and ready for the visitors I can already hear them cleaning out the fridge. If we don't get down there soon, we'll be eating bologna sandwiches for dinner."

"I doubt that, but it doesn't seem wise to risk it."

He smiled at her response as he helped her into the shower, giving the towel wrapped around her a gentle tug. Her surprised squeak made him chuckle despite the glare he caught her giving him over her shoulder.

"You should dial back the attitude, baby. You're off-balance and naked, I'd say that puts you at a distinct disadvantage."

"And I'll try to remember you said I didn't have anything you hadn't seen."

"It's true though yours holds far more appeal than what I see at the clinic. Those women don't tempt me.

You, on the other hand, would tempt a saint." He leaned against the wall, out of the mist, watching as she stepped under the spray. Bracing her hands against the granite wall, he heard her soft groan. Christ in heaven, he was going to have a permanent zipper tattoo along the length of his cock if he didn't rein in his raging libido.

London hadn't moved from where she stood leaning against the wall, but she didn't seem to need help, so he waited. Watching the water sluice down her petite frame was its own torture. After spending years dealing with his female patients as well as female submissives at the club, Evan was well acquainted with their tendency to focus on what they considered flaws rather than celebrating the beauty of the whole picture. He'd bet his considerable fortune, London was less than impressed with her curves— curves that were currently making his cock so hard, he wondered if there was any blood left in his damned brain.

"Are you going to stand there and stare the whole time I'm in here?" She hadn't lifted her head from where it rested against the marble wall, but she must have sensed his continued presence and scrutiny. He smiled to himself as the scent of her arousal drifted around him. Damn, his wolf was already clamoring for release, but he pushed back the temptation to make her his own.

"Yes." He had no intention of risking her safety by walking away. "Why would I leave you alone in a marble enclosure when I know you are teetering on the edge? Your safety will always be my priority, London." Another wave of scent hit him, and he felt his nostrils flare in response to the sweet smell of her honey. "And all that aside, I'm enjoying the view. You have a beautiful body, baby." He could practically hear the protests forming, and he had no plans to let her verbalize them.

"Be very careful what you say, sweetheart, because I'll take a very dim view of you disparaging yourself. As I see it, you are at a distinct disadvantage here." And wasn't that one of the biggest lies he'd ever told? Hell, she had every advantage in the world at this moment. The sound of a single sniff was all it took for him to kick off his boots and peel off his socks before tossing his shirt aside. He'd leave his jeans on, so he wasn't tempted to push her sweet curves against the wall and claim what he already knew was his. There would be plenty of time for that later, and once he started, Evan planned to spend hours exploring every inch of her.

Closing the distance between them with silent steps, he pulled her away from the wall and turned her, so they were face to face. The forlorn look in her eyes undid him.

"Come here, baby. Let me hold you for a minute." He was pleased when she took the initiative to close the small distance between them, laying her cheek against his chest and leaning close. "I've got you, baby. Let go."

His softly whispered words must have snapped the tenuous hold she had on her emotions because her whole body shuddered once, then again as the first sobs broke free. London's body trembled as all her fear bubbled to the surface. He absorbed as much of the negative emotions as he could while threading his fingers through her long hair in soothing strokes. Pumping shampoo into his hand, he massaged her tender scalp before easing his fingers through the long silken strands. With a little luck, he'd have her hair washed and conditioned by the time she realized what was happening. He only hoped she wouldn't be too emotionally and physically drained to talk to the men gathering downstairs.

He'd finished her hair as her hiccupping sobs slowed. When he felt her knees shaking against his legs, he moved her to the bench at the back of the shower. By the time he'd finished washing the smudges from her face and carefully cleaned the cuts she'd sustained, her lashes were feathered against the dark smudges under her eyes. Frowning at the evidence of her fatigue she'd hidden with makeup, Evan felt the protective instincts of his wolf roaring to life. *Fucking hell, she needs a damned keeper.*

Chapter Four

WALKING INTO A room filled with strangers was the very last thing London wanted to do, but she knew there was no way to avoid their questions. Looking down at her jeans and t-shirt, she shook her head and smiled. "I guess you were right about the Sheriff being able to get into my car." There'd been clothes sitting on Evan's dresser when they'd stepped from the shower, and she'd almost cried in relief.

"I think you'll find my community looks after their own, London." He must have seen her confusion reflected in her expression because he shook his head before she could protest.

Even though she had nine siblings, London had never felt she was fully a part of the group. She had always viewed the world through a scientific lens—things were true or false with little to no gray areas. Her siblings, on the other hand, saw the world in shocking shades of vibrant color, and the simple truth was they made her feel dowdy.

She'd dressed quickly and walked ahead of him as they moved down the hall leading to the main living area. Evan's arm encircled her, bringing her to a quick halt before pulling her into a nearby room. The room was completely devoid of light, but Evan obviously had no trouble seeing since he took two steps before abruptly stopping.

"What were you thinking about in the hallway, London? Don't think, just answer." His voice was almost coarse, the barely disguised growl simmering beneath the surface.

"I was thinking how plain I always feel in comparison to my siblings. They are so much more interesting…" She didn't finish the sentence because his hold on her tightened in warning, and she decided it was probably a good idea to stop before she dug the hole any deeper. She'd read enough about Dominants to know they frowned on women speaking negatively about themselves.

"You are wrong, and I'm going to enjoy helping you learn that lesson, baby. I think you've spent far too long hiding the adventurous spirit I know is at the heart of you. You use those insecurities as a shield when you are nervous, but when you are distracted and preoccupied, you are fearless and think nothing will hurt you." London sucked in a quick breath and was grateful for the darkness hoping it would hide her embarrassment. "God, I love that sweet blush. Even if I couldn't see it, I would be able to feel the heat radiating from your beautiful face."

Well shit, so much for hiding.

He turned her in his arms so quickly she would have stumbled if he hadn't fit her back firmly against his chest. "I don't want you walking into a room filled with members of my pack feeling as if you don't belong. You have every right to be here. I'm thrilled you called me when you needed help although I suspect you should have called much sooner." She was surprised he'd used the term pack but relieved to have her suspicions confirmed. Maybe her instincts about people weren't entirely off-base.

"I'm not sure there is anything I can do about being distracted. I often have trouble focusing unless I'm working, then I'm usually accused of being totally oblivious to my surroundings." Her tendency to neglect her own safety when working was one of the reasons Israel had agreed to assess the lab's security. He and Austin had both tried to persuade her to return to Texas, but she'd known how that would end… hell, she'd have been a virtual prisoner under their watch.

"I think I can help you focus, London. Are you willing to let me try?" Her body was responding before her mind processed the words, but he must have misinterpreted her hesitation. "The scent of your arousal gives you away, baby. Open your jeans for me."

Her breath caught, and despite knowing he could see too much in the pitch blackness surrounding them, she still found a small bit of comfort knowing she wasn't in full daylight.

London's fingers fumbled with the snap and zipper before her mind had a chance to voice all the usual warnings—*no reason to let common sense stand in the way of pleasure*. She didn't have enough experience to know what she might be missing, but London had read enough to know it wasn't something she wanted to forgo. There was no denying the chemistry between them, and if he could calm the storm in her mind for a few minutes, she would welcome the reprieve.

"Such a good girl. I'm going to reward your compliance, baby. Lean against me, I won't let you fall."

She wasn't sure why he thought she might fall, but being surrounded by his warmth fueled her desire in a way she hadn't expected. London had never experienced anything this intimate, and the sense of connection was an unexpected bonus. One arm encircled her torso below her breasts, lifting them as if they were an offering. Evan nuzzled his face against the still damp skin along her neck, and she moaned when the tip of his tongue snaked out to flick over the sensitive spot behind her ear.

"I'm going to enjoy mapping all your sweet spots, baby. All the places that make you moan and shudder in my arms are waiting to be discovered, but right now, I'm going to focus on giving you an orgasm that will settle your nerves." His hand slipped into her jeans, easily sliding beneath the elastic of her lace thong, gliding over the bare surface of her mound. "Fuck me, sweetheart. You're testing my control. When were you last waxed?" London smiled to herself, knowing he'd seen her bare mound in the shower, but he hadn't touched her, so the perfectly smooth skin had obviously been a pleasant surprise.

"No, I'm lasered. I waxed once and swore I'd never do it again." She had no idea how her sisters endured the pain of waxing, and when she'd said as much, they'd laughed and told her it was worth it. It had been her oldest sister, Asia, who'd pulled her aside and suggested she look into laser treatments, assuring her the process took several months to complete but more convenient than waxing, and the permanent results made it worth the time and money. Following Asia's advice, London had completed the treatments several months ago.

At Evan's first touch, London felt a heated rush of cream flood her vagina, coating the bare lips of her labia. His fingertips moved over the denuded surface, and her knees began shaking. The calloused tip of his finger circled her clit, and London felt Evan's arm tighten around her torso as her knees folded out from under her. Holy hell, her body felt like someone had started a fire in her core, the heat spreading to the surface so rapidly, London felt herself begin to tremble.

"Let it take you, baby. I promise to catch you. You'll always be safe in my arms, London." His reassurance was all it took for her to let the wave building deep inside crash through her. London felt as if a floodgate opened, and pleasure swamped her so quickly, she didn't have time to hold back her cry of pleasure. She was sure her heart was going to beat right out of her chest as she gasped for air and sagged in his hold.

"Oh. My. God. I had no idea." She felt his chest vibrate and heard something that sounded like a growl before she felt his teeth grazing along the top of her shoulder. When had he pulled her shirt aside?

"I can't wait to make love to you, baby. This was only a small taste of the pleasure I can give you."

If this was just an appetizer, London wasn't sure she would survive the main course. Her whole body felt relaxed, and she wondered how long it would be before her legs were strong enough to hold her up. Taking several deep breaths, she was startled to realize Evan had set her on her feet, and she was standing on her own.

"Come on. Let's get this over with. The sooner we get them out of here, the sooner we'll both be naked with my cock buried so deep inside you, neither of us knows where one ends, and the other begins."

Something about his crude words struck her as funny, and London felt a giggle bubble up before she could hold it back. She was pleased he hadn't taken offense at her ill-timed amusement.

"You'll find my community is very open about sex, baby. We may shock you at times, but once you embrace the freedom it gives you, I think you'll find it's a huge relief." London wasn't sure she would ever be able to speak so openly about sex, but she was too mellow now to argue the point.

After helping her fix her clothing and smooth her hair, Evan led her into the room where his friends were gathered. Everyone stopped talking as soon as they stepped into the large open area making up the kitchen and living room, causing London to stop dead in her tracks. The only movement in the room was the flaring of nostrils and knowing smiles spreading over the faces of the men who were making no attempt to hide their amusement. She looked at the group gathered in the large room and steeled herself against the overwhelming urge to flee.

***

"DAMNIT, WHAT THE hell is wrong with you? This is no way to treat an esteemed guest." Evan was instantly furious. Fucking hell, almost every person in the room knew how he felt about London Adler. Once he'd identified her as his mate, Evan had followed tradition and declared his intentions during a moonlight meeting of the elders.

Focusing his attention on his brother, Evan was surprised to see Eli's nostrils flare as heat reflected in his eyes. It was common for brothers in their pack to share a mate, but he and Eli had never considered it a possibility since they'd never been remotely attracted to the same type of woman. The Council of Elders and their parents had all pushed them to form a polyamorous union, but he and Eli hadn't even been able to agree on what they considered important in a mate.

Seeing the look in his brother's eyes, Evan smiled to himself. Knowing they'd found a woman they could agree on was more gratifying than he'd imagined. Possibilities swirled in his mind even as a surge of possessiveness hit him like a ton of bricks had been dropped on his chest. Hell, the idea of sharing had seemed a lot more appealing when it had been a nameless, faceless woman between them. Looking down at London, he wasn't surprised to see the anxiety creeping back into her expression. She was picking up the thick tension permeating the room, and that was the last thing he wanted. *Damn!*

"What the hell is wrong with you people? This is not how we treat guests, and it certainly isn't the way we treat one of our own." He knew the message wouldn't be lost on the members of his pack, but he could feel London stiffen beside him. Turning to her, he shook his head. "We'll talk about this later, sweetheart, but for now, suffice to say I apologize for the reception you've gotten. I swear they aren't as clueless about social niceties as they seem." Her muscles relaxed a fraction as they were surrounded by people offering their greetings, assuring her they hadn't meant to be rude.

Eli was the last to step up, moving in front of London to quietly introduce himself, pulling her small hand in between his own. Evan had never seen his brother in humble-mode and found himself biting back a grin.

"I'm pleased to meet you, London, although I wish it were under different circumstances. I'm Evan's brother Elijah, but please call me Eli." London's cheeks flushed, her breath shuddering when Eli's hands remained closed over hers.

Evan was inordinately pleased when she slowly pulled her hand from between his brother's and took a side step closer to him. He was willing to consider sharing, but he wasn't going to be denied tonight alone with her—he'd waited too long. Feeling her cream flow over his fingers a few minutes ago had been the sweetest form of torture. Her scent had pushed itself into his soul, making his wolf strain against the short leash he always kept it on when London was near.

Eli's eyes were dilated with arousal, but to his credit, he didn't press the issue by closing the small distance between them. Turning to the rest of the room, Eli asked everyone to introduce themselves, including why they were included in this particular meeting. Evan appreciated his brother adding the second piece of information. For London, knowing the connections would go a long way to making her feel more secure when sharing any sensitive information related to her research. As expected, Trinity stepped forward first. His size alone intimidated most people, so Evan was relieved London would find out there was a soft heart hidden behind the man's stern expression.

"I'm Trinity Frost though my friends call me Trin. I

was already on my way to the lab at Gates, responding to a report of gunfire when I got the call from Seth." His nod to the youngest man in the room had the newly appointed security officer blushing to the roots of his blonde hair. "I'm the local Sheriff, it was my office you parked in front of this morning. Your car has been secured, and I brought most of your personal belongings along—they are upstairs in one of the guest rooms, but I didn't unpack anything in case you want to move them." Evan bit back a grin because Trin already knew where London would be sleeping—that was why he'd brought a change of clothes into the master suite for her.

To her credit, London didn't respond other than to thank him for bringing her things and stepping forward to extend her hand. Trinity Frost was not only tall, he was also built like a linebacker, and his enormous hand nearly swallowed London's. Trin seemed to be taken by surprise by her gesture, but Evan saw newfound respect reflected in his cousin's eyes.

"I'm also cousin to these two," he gestured from Evan to Eli before continuing, "although I hope you won't hold that against me." Trin flashed her the smile Evan knew usually had women sliding out of their panties, but London appeared unaffected.

"I have nine brothers and sisters, Sheriff Frost, I'm the last person who would judge someone based on family." Trinity leaned his head back and laughed before nodding his understanding. Seth and Abe Keller introduced them-selves next, outlining their security duties at the clinic and the surrounding compound quickly and shaking London's offered hand. Axel Thorn moved closer, nodding at

London before smiling at his wife standing at his side.

"I'm Axel, and this is my wife, Mary Grace. I'm the head of security for the company owned businesses and land—that is to say, everything except for this compound. My lovely wife was with me when I got the call you'd been attacked, and she wasn't going to hear of me coming alone." Evan saw London's eyes widen, and he knew she'd gotten the wrong impression but also knew Dr. Mary Grace Thorn would clear things up quickly enough.

"I'm so happy to meet you, Dr. Adler. I've been looking forward to hearing all the details of your research since I first heard you were studying vaccines. As a pediatrician, I'm caught between a rock and a hard place without any substantive evidence linking vaccines and the prevalence of certain conditions. Shifters are a unique species; vaccines affect our children differently... but withholding them without revealing our true nature is very difficult." When Mary Grace finally paused long enough to take a breath, London seized the opportunity.

"I'd love to visit with you sometime. Perhaps Evan can help me arrange something. It sounds like you have observations that could be useful, and I will probably ask you a zillion questions if you're game."

Evan felt himself swell with pride. Damn, London was not only brilliant in the lab, but she was also a rock star when it came to making people feel valued. He doubted she really needed to hear Mary Grace's observations, but she'd just made an influential friend and won the heart of every man in the room with her kindness.

"Evan and I will coordinate schedules and make sure you ladies have a chance to visit in the next day or so."

Evan gave his brother a quick look of gratitude before smiling down at London. "Once your safety is assured, we'll arrange something at the main house. It will give Evan and me an opportunity to talk over a few things as well." Evan knew exactly what Eli wanted to discuss, and he was looking forward to the conversation but wasn't going to wait for a damned women's luncheon to have it. He wanted to have the chat as soon as possible—it was a discussion he'd worried they would never have.

Chapter Fi e

LONDON BARELY MANAGED to process the introductions after Eli Monroe's hands closed over hers. The electric current that raced up her arm at their first touch reminded her of the first time she'd met Evan. London's reaction to Evan seemed more significant because she'd felt it from across a crowded room, but she'd been shaken to her core by Elijah's as well. Maybe it was a false flag, given she was still catching her breath from the earth-shaking orgasm she'd had just minutes before walking into the room. That had to be it because if that wasn't the issue, she was seriously screwed up. *What sort of woman lets one brother finger fuck her into a stupor, then imagines the other one doing the same thing less than five minutes later?*

Everyone in the room seemed genuinely concerned about her safety, and it was reassuring to know the Sheriff had thought far enough ahead to bring her personal effects along. *At least it doesn't seem as though they plan to kick me to the curb anytime soon.* Hopefully, she could stay until she had a chance to call Austin. He'd make sure she was delivered safely home… and by home, she knew he'd mean his penthouse apartment atop the Adler Oil building in Austin. Groaning internally as she considered being sheltered in Austin's sterile palace, London wondered how long it would be before he strangled her... her siblings would probably start a pool to guess the date and hour.

Austin Adler had always been the most organized person London knew. Even with nine younger siblings, his bedroom had always been pristine. Nothing was ever out of place—his brothers and sisters had all known there would be hell to pay if they entered his domain without permission. How he'd enforced his privacy without ever lifting a finger remained a mystery, but he'd never had to do anything more than speaking the words aloud, and the rest of them had merely obeyed his commands. Now that she considered it, maybe calling him wasn't such a good idea.

Feeling Evan's arm tighten around her, London forced herself to focus on the man standing in front of her with his head tilted to the side as if waiting for her to respond.

"I'm sorry, could you repeat the question? I'm afraid my mind was drifting, and I missed it the first time." Sheriff Frost nodded as the corners of his mouth twitched.

"I asked if you have any idea who would want to hurt you."

"The list is probably reasonably long, starting with every large pharmaceutical manufacturer in the world. They don't know exactly what I'm working on, but the rumor mill would be enough to convince them a little collateral damage was justified in sustaining their bottom line." She sucked in a deep breath before letting her eyes move around the room as she tried to decide how much to reveal. Feeling safe with a group of people and being safe weren't always the same, and she'd learned the hard way—

she wasn't the best judge of character.

"Dr. Adler, I assure you anything you say in this room will be held in strict confidence. The nature of our community and the safety of our kind depends on our ability to keep our mouths shut." Trinity Frost's simple declaration rang true. She knew how carefully her brothers guarded their secret and it made sense these people would face the same dangers.

As a chemist, London knew how ruthless scientists could be when backed against a wall, forced to explain anyone or anything deemed different. Scientists would dissect until they uncovered and documented every fact, and they wouldn't give a tinker's damn who they hurt in the process.

"Point taken. Without going into a lot of boring details and conjecture, I'll say this... big pharma makes billions on vaccines. They have convinced the world the inoculations are necessary even when they know they're not. American taxpayers are being sold a load of horse apples, and to add insult to injury, they are funding the whole smoke and mirrors campaign through the Centers for Disease Control. They not only encourage the vaccination overload, but they have also lobbied until all fifty states demand compliance." She stopped to take a breath and realized she was preaching rather than providing the information they'd asked for.

"I'm sorry, that was way more information than you needed. Suffice to say, my research is not only going to prove they are using vaccines to boost profits, but I've uncovered links between vaccines and several different diseases later in life. The details will turn science on its ear and will devastate several of the biggest players in the field."

She suddenly realized the danger she'd put them in by calling Evan for help and felt her shoulders drop in resignation. This group, more than any other, didn't need the unnecessary attention she would bring them. Looking to her side, London focused on Evan.

"I'm sorry. I shouldn't have called you. This is going to bring needless trouble to you and your family. Hell, I can't even give you a good description of the man shooting up the lab because he was wearing a mask." His eyes narrowed, and he shook his head.

"I swear if you say one more word along this line, I'm going to paddle your perfect ass. As far as I'm concerned, your mistake was not calling sooner."

She sucked in a quick breath but didn't respond. She'd been dealing with Alpha-men her whole life, so she was no stranger to knowing when to exercise her right to remain silent.

"I'm guessing she's been worried for a while since she'd already packed her car and moved it into town." The Sheriff took a step forward and crossed his bulging arms over his chest. The move was meant to be intimidating—it might have been if she hadn't seen her brothers use the same thing more times than she cared to count. *You're going to have to do better than that, Sheriff.*

"You might want to try a new approach, fellas because Dr. Adler doesn't seem like a woman you're going to be able to buffalo. I'll bet she's encountered testosterone before." Mary Grace had just been promoted to London's BFF, and she gave the other woman a smile of thanks.

"I don't want her to run because she thinks we can't keep her safe, the ass-wipes after her are more than we can handle, or some misguided attempt to protect us."

Looking into Evan's eyes, London saw the same golden highlights she'd seen sparkling in her brothers' eyes when they'd been holding on to their control by a thread. Those looks were usually reserved for Asia, Brooklyn, Catalina, or Paris because London had done her best to avoid conflict with her brothers. She hadn't felt any particular obligation to get along with them, rather it felt like she'd usually used up all her *family grace* by arguing with her parents at every turn.

"It's not that I don't trust you… I think I proved it… after all, you were the first person I thought of when I knew there was someone in the lab. I'd already dialed your number when the masked man started shooting. And speaking of his shooting, he is either the world's worst shot, or he wasn't trying to kill me. He had a clear shot more than once but always shot above my head or far enough to the side, the only way he could have hit me was for me to launch myself into his line of fire."

London watched Sheriff Frost's eyes widen in surprise before his expression darkened into a scowl. "Are you saying you think he was just trying to scare you? What purpose would *that* serve? Unless someone was waiting in the wings to ride in and save the day."

London felt her cheeks heat, a reaction every man in the room seemed to zero in on. She only knew one man who would set up something like this.

Evan looked like he was a hot minute away from going over the edge into apocalyptic, making her take an instinctive step back, finding herself pressed against Eli's warm chest, his left arm wrapping around her torso just beneath her breasts. Since the good Sheriff hadn't seen fit to deliver anything more substantial than a lace bra, Eli's move highlighted her rapidly peaking nipples. *Geez, London, get a damned grip on your libido.*

Their significant difference in height was both intimidating and comforting, making her wonder how many steps she'd have to stand on to look Evan and Elijah in the eye. Her mind flashed to a scene where she was naked between the two of them, their hands moving over her sweat-dampened skin as her head thrashed from side to side, lost in pleasure so intense, she was convinced she wouldn't survive it.

London didn't realize she'd closed her eyes until Eli's lips brushed over the shell of her ear, bringing her back to the moment, despite the soft moan that escaped before she could hold it back. Blinking her eyes, she focused on Evan who stood much closer now, his eyes glittering with golden flecks and heat. Eli's arm tightened as he spoke, his warm breath caressing the sensitive skin behind her ear.

"Who? We want a name, love." London's knees were dangerously close to folding out from under her. She knew Eli wouldn't let her fall, but she hated feeling so vulnerable.

Geez Louise, fuzzy, fucking bunnies have more restraint than I do. Hell, she'd been lost in a sexual fantasy so hot, she could feel the cream soaking the engorged folds of her pussy. Her breathing was shallow, and she'd been on a fast-track to release while being questioned by local law enforcement and surrounded by virtual strangers. What the hell was wrong with her? It was if she'd lost control of her own body. When had she become a damned hormone driven teenager?

"Franklin Cordesi." London felt the tension in the room ratchet up at the mention of Franklin's name, but she wasn't sure why the air seemed to be crackling around her.

ELI HAD SEEN his brother's frustration, and anticipating London's reaction, he'd moved silently into position behind her. She stepped back when she saw Evan's expression and feeling her pressed solidly against him for the first time sent a surge of his blood directly to his cock. For the first time in years, Eli worried his wolf was going to break free—hell, he hadn't spontaneously shifted since he first reached puberty.

London's scent seeped so deep inside him, Eli knew he'd never forget this moment. Her soft curves molded against him perfectly, and he felt her body shift closer when he whispered against the shell of her ear. He'd love to know where her mind had gone. He'd felt her body temperature spike, and the sweet smell of her cream filled the air around them. Evan stepped forward, the frustration erased from his expression, replaced by pure heat.

Fucking hell, it was going to be torture leaving her tonight, but he knew his brother as well as he knew himself, and there was no way in hell Evan was going to give up having her to himself. His brother had been waiting far too long for this opportunity. Since he and Evan grew up with two dads, they understood the importance of resolving challenges without involving their mate, so this would be settled out of her hearing. Their mom had always told anyone who would listen how blessed she felt knowing she didn't have to choose a side in a disagreement, nor had she ever felt any guilt about spending time alone with either of her husbands.

Eli and Evan were going to have a long talk about Dr. London Adler in the very near future, but for now, ensuring her safety would have to be enough. The name she'd given them sounded vaguely familiar, but Eli would wait until the report came in before making any decisions. If the man was responsible for the attack on London at the lab, it wouldn't matter what connections he had to the pack, Franklin Cordesi had signed his own death warrant as far as Eli was concerned.

FRANKLIN CORDESI LEANED back against the supple black leather of his chair and sighed. He should have taken care of the job himself instead of agreeing to let one of his underlings handle it. He'd worried London might recognize him even with his face hidden by a mask—she was too observant to miss even the slightest hint of familiarity in movement. Franklin wasn't sure he'd ever met anyone as bright as London Adler, nor had he met a woman more unaware of her appeal.

What had started out as an assignment had quickly morphed into something much more, but the day she'd confronted him with the damned file some busybody sent her, she hadn't been interested in his explanation. London had shown him what she received, then walked away. No tears, no arguments—she'd just turned and walked out, but not before he'd seen the humiliation and hurt in her eyes. Knowing he'd hurt her felt like a knife to his heart, but she hadn't given him a chance to explain how his feelings had changed. She'd blocked his number and email address. Hell, as far as he could tell, she was only accepting calls from her family. He'd tried using alias accounts, but it hadn't mattered—every attempt was met with silence.

He'd planned to have his man scare her, driving her out the front of the building and right into his waiting arms. It would have been easy for her to believe he was coming to see her since she'd been avoiding him for several weeks. It had appeared to be a foolproof plan—except for one detail. Franklin hadn't known she had contacts nearby, and that lapse proved how desperate he'd been to convince her he considered her more than a means to an end. Christ, what a clusterfuck. Now, she might as well be hidden in fucking Fort Knox. It had taken him most of the night to hack enough local security feeds to figure out who'd rescued London from the wooded area behind the lab, but he'd finally succeeded in getting a picture of a black pickup.

Once he had a description of the truck racing toward the Gates' facility, it hadn't taken long to identify the owner and connect the dots. Dr. Evan Monroe had treated London's sister a few months ago, but he suspected they could have already known each other, considering they both worked in medical professions. What he didn't know was where she was now. He assumed there was a second entrance into the compound surrounding Monroe's clinic, but since there were no cameras in the area, he was left wondering. The damned truck couldn't have disappeared into thin air.

Franklin sent a couple of his men to explore the area, but they'd been met at the highway entrance by two deputies who'd explained they were investigating an attack at Gates, and the surrounding area was off-limits for the foreseeable future. *What the fuck does that mean? How long did they plan to restrict access?* He knew it wasn't a public access road, but it wasn't marked as private either. The gravel lane was used more than most people realized since it led to a small lake favored by the locals for fishing and family outings.

If Evan Monroe picked London up, as Franklin suspected, it seemed reasonable he'd taken her to his clinic. The last security footage of her showed her clothing had been shredded by falling glass, but he hadn't been able to determine how badly she'd been injured. It didn't seem likely she was badly hurt since he hadn't seen any of the doctor's staff entering the facility until the next morning for what was likely business as usual. He could only hope he hadn't hurt her physically as well as emotionally. *Fucking hell, this seemed so simple when it all started.*

Chapter Six

LONDON WAS DEAD on her feet. She'd answered every question the small group had thrown at her even those she knew had nothing to do with the attack at the lab. Evan and Eli both asked questions about her relationship with Franklin, and she'd seen the relief in their eyes when she explained they'd only gone on a handful of dates.

She and Franklin had dated less than a month, and their relationship never progressed past going to dinner and attending a movie. *Cripes, Franklin didn't even kiss me until the last two times we went out.* He'd expressed an interest in her work and listened attentively as she bemoaned how difficult it was to find competent lab help who couldn't be bought. It was humiliating how easily she'd been taken in, and it had been emotionally draining to admit her naivety to the small group who were now charged with keeping her safe.

Mary Grace had given her a hug before leaving and reminded her looking for the best in people was not a character flaw. "You'll find your faith in people will be rewarded in our community." London wasn't entirely sure what her new friend meant but appreciated the other woman's attempt to make her feel better.

Eli had been the last one to leave, and London wished she'd have been able to decipher the silent communication that seemed to pass between the brothers. When he hugged her goodbye, promising to see her the next day, she'd been surprised how right it felt to be in his arms. When she finally stepped back out of Eli's embrace, London had been surprised to see nothing but heat in Evan's gaze. She saw the same desire in Elijah's as the door closed between them and worried she was on a slippery slope. The last thing she needed was to cause trouble between the Monroe brothers... no one would win, and she'd be left with her reputation in tatters and without either of them in her life.

Swaying as fatigue threatened to drop her like a stone, London squeaked in surprise as Evan lifted her into his arms.

"Baby, you were a heartbeat from crashing. I expect you to take better care of yourself." There was a compelling tone in his voice she found both annoying and comforting, but she was too tired to argue. Leaning her head against his shoulder, she let him carry her up the stairs and down the hall to his bedroom. She knew she should sleep in the guest room, but there was still a small part of her worried about being alone.

"I should probably—" She was prevented from finishing when his finger pressed against her lips.

"You'll sleep in my bed, London. I've waited too long for this moment." His words shocked her, and London felt her eyes widen in surprise. "You have to know how much I want you, baby. I knew you were mine from the moment our eyes locked at the conference and feeling you come apart in my arms a few hours ago sealed the deal. Your sweet cream soaking my fingers was both perfection and agony. I wanted nothing more than to push myself so deep, you'd think we were one."

His hands slipped under the hem of her shirt, sliding up until he was able to toss it aside. When she instinctively moved to cover her lace covered breasts, he shook his head.

"Don't ever hide yourself from me, baby. These pretty pink nipples peeking through the lace have tormented me since you pulled the shirt on. I'm going to make a note to thank Trin for including sexy underwear when he brought your clothes into the bedroom." She felt her knees weaken and locked them to keep from melting into a puddle at his feet. "Make no mistake, Trinity didn't randomly choose your bra and panties—he, like every other Dominant I know, considers them a pleasant decoration but an unnecessary distraction—it's a wonder he didn't conveniently *forget* to include them. Having unimpeded access to what Doms consider *theirs* is second only to the safety and happiness of the submissive in their care." Threading his fingers into her hair on each side of her face, Evan's large hands tilted her head back until she was looking into his eyes.

"Your safety will always be my number one priority, London. If you entrust yourself to me, I'll move heaven and earth to keep you safe and ensure your happiness." Without giving her a chance to respond, he pressed his lips against hers, the rush of heat racing through London's veins fading the fatigue until it was barely remembered. When she lifted her arms to wrap them around Evan's neck, he pulled back and shook his head.

"Keep your arms at your sides, baby. My control is hanging by a thread. Your touch will snap it, and I'll ravage you."

Her sex was pulsing with need, making thoughts of being ravaged sound like a great idea if you asked her… maybe the best idea she'd ever heard. When he pulled her arms behind her back, shackling her wrists with one hand, she felt her pussy flood with cream, and a moan vibrated deep in her throat.

"The scent of your desire is seeping into my soul, baby, and knowing how you've responded to this small taste of bondage pleases me more than I can tell you. I'm looking forward to seeing you bound to my bed, spread open for my exploration and pleasure." London had the impression he'd wanted to say more, but he'd held back, and she found herself worrying about what he hadn't said.

"I don't know what you are thinking about, sweetheart, but I'm going to make it my goal to erase every troubling thought from your mind tonight."

She wasn't sure she could turn off her brain, God only knew she'd never had any luck before. There had been times in her life she'd considered her intelligence a curse because it didn't seem like there was never an opportunity to escape. London had been so lost in her thoughts, she hadn't realized she was now standing naked in front of the man she hadn't been able to stop thinking about since the first time they met. *Where in the hell did my jeans and thong go?*

She heard Evan chuckle and looked up at him in confusion.

"I may need to reconsider helping you focus, you are awfully easy to deal with when you are lost in thought." She glared at Evan making him laugh out loud. "Oh, baby, you better dial back that look. I assure you Elijah will take issue with that cute glare—but that's a discussion we'll have later. Tonight is all about your pleasure." She must have looked as confused as she felt because he grinned. "Don't look so befuddled, baby. Your pleasure feeds mine."

London didn't have enough experience to fully understand what Evan meant, but she kept her uncertainty to herself. *People have been having sex since the dawn of mankind; surely, I'll be able to figure it out. How hard can it be?*

EVAN LOOKED INTO London's eyes and felt his heart squeeze with something more than desire, but he wasn't willing to call it love—not yet. He'd been raised by pack leaders, so he understood as well as anyone the significance of mating. Every pack had their own rules, and their group was no different. Some shifters knew their mates solely by scent. He'd heard stories about shifters following a scent for miles to find the one the Universe had chosen for them. There were also packs whose mating rituals were much more similar to non-shifters—they met and built a relationship over time.

The members of Evan's pack fell somewhere in between—they relied heavily on scent, believing the chemistry between mates was easily identified. Oddly enough, his and Eli's responses to London had been triggered by eye contact first, but he certainly wasn't going to discount the significance of scent. His response to the smell of her skin was building to a crescendo as his tongue pushed into her sweet mouth. Her tongue slid along his in a dance as old as time, teasing and tempting as surely as if she were dancing naked on the table. Growling deep in his throat, he pulled her against him, knowing she would feel the steel length of his cock pressing against her bare torso.

The difference in their heights would present a few challenges, but nothing he couldn't handle—and nothing he and Eli couldn't easily overcome together. Ordinarily, Evan would turn her, so she was on all fours, but he'd made a significant discovery when he'd used his fingers to bring her to climax before the meeting. His sweet London was a virgin. It might make him old-fashioned, but in his opinion, her trust, innocence, and children were the greatest gifts a woman could give a man.

Evan was humbled to know she'd chosen him, and it was a treasure he would hold in his heart forever—it also meant he wanted to make love to her face to face. Being able to see her expression and look into her eyes would help him gauge how she was coping. He wasn't a small man, he needed to know she was well prepared and ready to take him—tearing her delicate tissues was not an option. Evan would chew off his own arm before he'd hurt her.

"Before we go any further, I want you to know I'm clean. I have current test results I'll be happy to share." She nodded, letting him know she understood, and he noted the pink flush of embarrassment staining her cheeks. It would take time for her to adapt to the pack's openness—none of them were modest, embarrassment an emotion that had no place in their lives.

"I'm clean as well. I have to be tested because of my work in the lab, but the paperwork is in my car. I'm a… well, I haven't had sex since my last test. I'm on the pill… damn, I wonder where those are?" When she tried to push past him, he grasped her shoulders and shook his head.

"You can look for them later, baby. It won't make any difference if you take it now or in a few hours." He didn't bother to tell her he already knew she wasn't fertile. He'd be able to tell by the difference in her scent. Hell, every shifter in the pack would know when she was in season if they were close enough, but Evan and Eli would be able to tell from a far greater distance once they'd claimed her. Evan also kept quiet that her birth control prescription would be ineffective against a shifter pregnancy, anyway. Trailing the side of his finger over her cheek, he watched her eyes dilate at the simple touch. He could hear the shift in her breathing and relished the spike he saw in her pulse pounding at the base of her throat.

"I don't want anything between us, London. I want to feel every inch of your silken heat wrapping around my cock and every quiver of your vaginal walls as your body surrenders to mine. I want to know what it feels like when your sweet cream slides like warm honey over my bare cock as your pleasure peaks and orgasm overtakes you." He was pleased to hear her breathing hitch and the pulse at the base of her neck kick up several more notches. Hell, at this rate she was going to come before he even started. Brushing his lips gently over hers, Evan loved seeing how swollen they were from their earlier passionate kisses and couldn't help envisioning how they would look wrapped around his cock.

Taking a step back, Evan let his eyes wander over London's sweet curves. She would never be model thin, and he was grateful. He'd never seen the appeal of making love to a stick. London Adler was pure perfection in his view—breasts that filled his hands and lush hips he'd be able to grasp as he fucked her from behind. Her muscular legs would wrap themselves around him, pushing his cock deeper as she arched beneath him. She'd lost too many pounds since he'd seen her months ago, but she would blossom back to a healthy weight under their care.

"On the bed, baby, spread your arms and legs wide. I want to admire the view while I undress." He knew the position would make her feel vulnerable, but he was anxious to see how she reacted to being displayed for his pleasure. Evan was looking forward to seeing her naked and spread wide while he and Eli watched television. They'd lay her out on the coffee table wide open, so they could watch cream coat the glistening folds of her pussy. He'd love watching her fingers stroke her clit until she was seconds away from release. Neither he nor Eli would let her come without one of them touching her—her orgasms would belong to them.

London moved into place, but he could see her legs inching back together as vulnerability started to overshadow desire. "Move your legs farther apart, baby. I want to see everything." She moved back into position, but it was easy to see what it cost her. "Fuck me, you are beautiful. I'm going to explore every inch of you, map each sweet spot, and lap at your pink folds until you're begging me to take you." He undressed as he spoke. Watching her eyes widen when his cock sprang free of its confines had been a huge ego boost.

"Ummm… I don't think this is going to work. I haven't… well, I haven't ever had sex… I haven't had sex with anyone with such a big…" London's eyes were wide, and he was picking up the tangy scent of fear as she stuttered her concern. Evan moved over her and silenced her with a blistering kiss. He was relieved to feel her body go lax beneath him and kissed his way to the sensitive spot behind her ear before moving down to press his tongue over the pulse point pounding just beneath her skin.

His wolf pushed for release as his lips skimmed over the junction where her neck met her shoulder—the spot where he would sink his teeth as his wolf claimed her was a magnet to the beast inside him. Grazing his teeth along the short expanse of skin, Evan waged an epic battle in his effort to resist the temptation. It was too soon to claim her, and if she agreed to a polyamorous relationship, he and Eli would want her between them when she became theirs.

Evan continued trailing butterfly kisses lower until he was able to circle one tight nipple with his tongue as his fingers pinched the other. London's startled gasp as she arched into his touch was all the encouragement he needed to continue.

"I can't wait to see your nipples in clamps, baby. Your body responds perfectly to a small bite of pain." He moved his hand slowly down over her flat belly until his fingers were skimming the smooth skin of her mound.

"The bare skin over your pussy is so fucking soft, it makes my cock even harder than it was before." When his fingers slipped between her slick folds, Evan groaned. "Fuck me, baby, you're soaked. I can hardly wait to get you into my playroom." A fresh wash of cream coated his fingers, and he growled deep in his throat.

"Please. I need… I need more."

He could feel her body lifting into his touch. He didn't make her wait, pushing two fingers inside, scissoring them several times before pulling back when her vaginal wall started fluttering.

"Not yet, baby, hold off as long as you can. I want the tip of my cock pressed against your cervix when you come." He wanted her to feel every pulse as he came deep inside her, and he wanted to feel her rippling around him, squeezing him as tightly as possible. He smiled against her quivering folds when she whimpered in protest.

"How am I supposed to hold back? I don't know how to do any of this, Evan."

He'd wondered if she would admit her inexperience. He'd never understood why women often considered their virginity a liability, but then he didn't understand men who refused to fuck a woman who wasn't experienced either.

"Baby, I already know this is new to you, and I can't tell you how much that pleases me. Teaching you all the ways you can experience pleasure is an enormous honor." It would also take the rest of their lives, but he didn't think she was ready to hear those words yet.

Moving up until the tip of his cock was poised at her entrance, he shifted his hips just enough to push the throbbing head into her heat. Biting the inside of his cheek, trying to maintain control, Evan sucked in a deep breath and mentally reviewed the periodic table of elements to distract himself from the pleasure swamping his senses. Fucking hell, he wanted to shove in balls deep, but he knew she wasn't ready.

"Now. Please. I need you inside me." The desperation in London's voice called to his wolf, and it took everything Evan had to hold back.

"We're going to take it nice and slow, baby. I want this to be an experience you remember fondly for the rest of your life, and you won't if I don't make sure your body is properly prepared." As he'd been speaking, Evan had been pushing forward, then retreating, gaining small increments with each thrust. "You are so fucking hot, you're burning me alive. And you are so tight, I'm barely hanging on." He'd asked her to hold back her orgasm, but now he was the one struggling to restrain himself. He pushed against the barrier and paused. Looking in London's eyes, he saw a mixture of hesitancy and desire, what he didn't see was fear.

"Are you ready, baby? It's only going to hurt for a few seconds, then the pain will be a distant memory." Ordinarily, he required spoken answers, but he accepted London's quick nod and pushed through. Her gasp and the single tear that escaped made his heart clench. Leaning down, he kissed the salty trail. "The pain is over, sweetheart. Take a deep breath and focus on the pleasure." The coppery scent of blood circled around him, and his wolf clamored for release. A few licks of his tongue would erase all remnants of her pain, but he wanted to make love to her as a man before she was exposed to the raw power of mating.

It took several more torturous minutes before he was fully seated, his tip pressed against the entrance to her womb. Taking a deep breath, Evan looked down at London and smiled.

"Your muscles are trying to pull me deeper, but my tip is already pressed against your cervix." He needed a minute to regain control, but her soft mewing was more than he could bear. Pulling back, he lifted himself up enough to see the faint streaks of blood smeared over the surface of his cock. Great Goddess and Sweet Mother Earth, he must be a fucking caveman—seeing the evidence of his claim to her innocence made him want to beat his fists against his chest in triumph.

"Oh, God. It feels so good. I always wondered, but now I understand."

No, baby. You don't understand yet, but you will. Setting a slow pace, Evan began making love to London, focusing all his attention on reading each of her body's responses. Her bright blue eyes slowly darkened until they were the most beautiful shade of violet he'd ever seen. Her pulse pounded beneath the surface, and her breaths became little more than pants. Evan had never fucked a woman without a condom, and the feel of her cream sliding over his bare cock was shredding his control.

"Wrap your legs around me, baby." She didn't hesitate and immediately moaned as he pressed against her G-spot. "Hang on, baby, we're going to kick this up a notch." Setting a fast pace, he waited until he knew they'd both passed the point of no return before speaking against her ear. "Now, London. Come for me, love." Her body was already responding to the command before he finished speaking.

London screaming his name as she climaxed around him was the sweetest sound he'd ever heard. As soon as she let go, he followed her over the edge into a soaring state of bliss—the most intense release he'd ever experienced. Evan had enough sexual experience to recognize the difference between this sexual experience and every other encounter. Hell, he'd seen stars bursting behind his eyelids and was forced to lock his elbows to keep from collapsing onto her. It took him a few seconds to pull himself together enough to speak.

"Damn, baby, you just stole a piece of my soul." And it was true, he'd never come so hard in his life. His parents all swore he and his brother shouldn't rely solely on scent to identify their mate. The three of them insisted they'd recognize her and know for sure they'd found *the one* when they felt their souls fuse together. Evan had never taken the advice seriously—until now. Rolling to his back, Evan kept London wrapped in his arms, so she was now lying sprawled over him like a warm blanket.

"I'll move if my arms and legs ever start working again." Her voice was barely audible even to his enhanced hearing. "You turned my brain to mush. All those years of college wasted. My siblings will probably have me committed to a funny farm where I can sit blubbering nonsense and staring blankly out the window all day, occasionally mumbling about my one sexual encounter."

Evan couldn't hold back his chuckle. Hell, in all the times he'd talked to London, he'd never seen any hint of a sense of humor—she'd always been all business.

"I'm sure your brain will come back online soon enough, sweetness. No need to worry about squandered scholarship dollars and years spent with your nose buried in textbooks." He didn't make any attempt to hide the amusement from his voice. Evan was happy she'd let her guard down enough to give him a glimpse of the real London. "That brilliant mind of yours would be a terrible thing to waste."

Truer words had never been spoken.

Chapter Se en

ELI LOOKED DOWN at the phone resting in the center of his desk and shook his head, wondering if London realized yet it was missing. Evan slipped the ancient device into his pocket as he'd been leaving, quietly asking him to check it for recent messages and calls. What Eli discovered left him in stunned disbelief. London had been dealing with what appeared to be several jerks, who not only posted their speculation about her research on social media but also sent personal messages when their public thrashings failed to get a response. Her patience and professionalism impressed him even as he fought the temptation to track the rude fuckers down.

Shaking his head, he wondered why she was using the outdated—by nearly a decade—technology. Hell, the device itself was so old, it had taken him hours to find a charger for the damned thing. He'd already bought her a new one and would make sure she knew how to use it when he saw her later today. He'd been pleased to see she'd blocked Franklin Cordesi's number. It had given Eli enormous pleasure to change Cordesi's number to auto-matically forward to his own secure line. When the man called late last night, he'd been quite surprised when Eli answered.

The report on Cordesi wasn't in yet, but knowing he'd thrown the other man off his game had been damned gratifying. Cordesi claimed he'd heard through mutual friends London had been attacked, and he was concerned about her safety. When Eli refused to divulge anything other than London was fine, the man grew annoyed and disconnected the call. Eli remembered where he'd heard Cordesi's name—he'd met him once several years earlier when the pack had been trying to purchase a neighboring tract of land. Cordesi provided the sellers with an inflated appraisal, and it had taken Eli several weeks to set things right. There was no doubt the man was money driven.

The next call had been from London's sister, Brooklyn who'd been worried sick about what she'd seen in her mind's eye. His conversation with Brooklyn hadn't lasted long because Luke Grayson had *persuaded* his frantic sub to relinquish the phone with a promise to paddle her ass if she didn't hand it over. Eli was still struggling to hold back his laughter and was certain B, as her family called her, was likely draped over her Master's lap at this moment, getting the punishment she so richly deserved.

Luke Grayson had called Austin Adler shortly after their conversation, and the eldest Adler immediately dialed his sister's phone to speak with Eli. As the business leaders of their respective packs, the two men had met on several occasions, but this was the first time their paths had crossed on a personal issue. In the beginning, Austin's questions centered on London's health and safety but had quickly shifted to his plans to move her to Texas before Eli interrupted.

"We're perfectly capable of keeping London safe, Austin. My brother and I will spare no expense protecting her." There was a long moment of silence before he heard Austin sigh.

"Does London know about this?" Eli didn't have to ask what Austin was referring to. The family patriarch wanted to be sure his sister wasn't being taken advantage of—and if their positions were reversed, Eli would feel the same way.

"It's a conversation we intend to have as soon as possible. Without going into details no brother wants to hear, I'll just say she's fully aware there is a strong attraction she can't explain. My brother has been in love with London for a long time, I met her yesterday. I want to assure you, we'll respect her decision—safe, sane, and consensual is more than a guiding tenet in the clubs we attend, it's one of the principles we live by, Mr. Adler." There had been a pregnant pause before Adler responded.

"Good to know. Please have my sister call me at her earliest convenience. I'll caution you, I'm not going to be the last Adler you're going to speak to tonight, Mr. Monroe, but I will do you a favor and stagger the messages to my siblings, so you aren't inundated with calls all at once." After a short pause, Eli heard the Austin chuckle on the other end of the line. "Hell, I'm not sure I'm helping much by ensuring you get calls all night long. Who the hell knows what time zone Israel and Cat are in, and Paris is a typical college kid, I swear she has no sense of time at all." This time it was Eli's turn to laugh, and he was grateful for the other man's attempt to lighten the mood.

"Understood. It's not a problem. I'll stay up as long as it takes to put everyone's mind at ease." He waited a moment before adding, "London is working on the assumption the man she dated briefly is behind the attack because from all appearances it was intended to frighten rather than harm her. His name is Franklin Cordesi, and she mentioned someone anonymously sent her information indicating the man was working for a consortium of pharmaceutical companies who have been trying to recruit her. She confronted him, and he acknowledged that was the way it was *in the beginning*, but when he tried to explain further, she simply walked away and blocked him from her phone and email."

"That sounds exactly like London. She's very black and white—loyal to a fault, but you only get one chance with her. Something you'd do well to remember, Elijah." Eli understood the warning, but it was unnecessary. The last thing he wanted to do was hurt London. He wanted to claim her, protect her from anyone who intended her harm, and make certain she had everything she needed to continue her vital work—he'd cut off his own hand before hurting her.

"I'll ask Israel to look into Cordesi, then coordinate with you—I assume you have your team on this as well."

"I do." And his team would have a report on his desk before Austin Adler could contact his brother. One of the first things he'd done when he returned home was direct his team to locate each member of London's family—he'd wanted to be sure none of them were close enough to swoop in and pull her away from them.

Over the next few hours, each of her siblings either called or sent a text message, all with similar concerns for her safety. Eli had answered each call and replied to every message, assuring London's brothers and sisters she was fine and would contact them at her earliest convenience.

Her phone was finally silent, and he used the opportunity to check her browsing history. Shaking his head at how easy it had been to figure out her password, he scrolled back through several months and smiled. Perhaps Dr. Adler was going to be more receptive to a poly-relationship and kink than he'd dare hope. It looked like she'd been researching dominance and submission, even checking out the sites of several nearby clubs. He and Evan would see to it their lovely sub didn't try to attend any of the munches he knew the clubs hosted monthly. Hell, she'd be a lamb lost in a pack of wolves—literally.

If she was interested in D/s, it might not be as difficult as he'd expected to convince her a relationship with two men would have its advantages. He'd already made a mental list of reasons it would be in her best interest, including his and Evan's demanding work schedules, their commitment to keeping her safe, and bone-melting sex.

Going back further in her browser history, Eli shook his head when he encountered tabloid articles about Evan's past relationships. His brother might be dedicated to his clinic now, but his close dealings with the rich and famous had garnered his personal life some unwanted attention once the exclusive clinic became successful.

Setting the phone in the top drawer of his desk, Eli turned the hidden dial, locking the drawer before leaving the room. Stepping out of his clothes near the back door, he stretched his arms over his head and smiled as he thought about how London would likely react to his pack's laissez-faire attitude about nudity. Being naked was not seen as a moral issue and certainly didn't elicit any embarrassment among pack members.

The weather was perfect, and the full moon highlighted the beauty surrounding him. Eli had planned to attend the claiming ceremony of three pack members but had been busy answering calls and hated knowing he'd probably already missed most of the ritual mating. Leaping over the railing, he'd fully shifted before his feet hit the thick grass.

Long looping strides took him to the edge of the woods, and in just a few seconds, he stood at the periphery of a large circle, watching as two of the younger members of the pack claimed a non-shifter they'd met in college. The young woman was so lost in pleasure, she appeared to have forgotten they were being watched by so many members of their community. Public claiming was common but not required.

Trin moved to stand beside Eli and nodded his head to the side, indicating his need to speak privately. Walking back to the outer border of the woods, both men shifted back into their human forms.

"I'm surprised to see you here, I figured you'd go back to Evan's as soon as you snooped through Dr. Adler's phone."

"Has anybody ever pointed out what a tactless bastard you are?" Eli shook his head at the other man's blunt assessment. It wasn't that he hadn't given plenty of thought to returning to Evan's, but he'd promised himself he'd give his brother one night alone with London—and he'd been determined to see it through.

"I checked out the lab at Gates, but it was a damned

battle to get in." Eli raised a brow at his friend's words. "Let's go back to your office and talk." Eli nodded before they both shifted to sprint the short distance back to the main house. At the edge of the yard, they split apart, Eli heading back to his private wing as Trinity veered to the right. One wing of the large mansion had rooms for short-term visitors among the apartments for those who lived onsite. He'd heard pack members refer to the vast wing as a combination apartment complex, bed-and-breakfast, and exclusive resort. The expansive space contained a well-equipment gym with large lockers where many club members left their clothing when they wanted to run in the woods or attend a celebration like the one held every full moon.

Eli was staring blankly into the commercial sized re-frigerator in the main kitchen when Trinity walked in. "Are you looking for something to eat or just taking inventory before the hoard descends?" Eli chuckled and pulled out large platters of meat and cheese, handing them to Trinity to set on the nearby bar.

"We'd better get a head start, or there won't be anything left. I don't remember the three of us eating as much as the younger guys do now. Christ, I don't know how the cooks keep up." And it was nothing less than the truth. They'd finally negotiated with the nearby grocery to have most of the food drop-shipped from their supplier—the privately owned store still got a large portion of their percentage, but no longer had to stock the shelves, and the cooks didn't have to make several trips to town every week.

Trinity shook his head and laughed. "You have to be

kidding. Hell, we nearly ate our parents out of house and home. To hear my mom tell it, they couldn't wait until our appetites slowed down."

Eli remembered his parents teasing them about cleaning out the fridge, but he was anxious to change the subject. It never took him long to tire of idle chit-chat. If he was going to have any self-control when he saw London in a few hours, he needed to get a couple hours of sleep.

"Why was it difficult to get into Gates?" When Trin shook his head at Eli's abrupt tone, Eli gave him a rueful smile. "Bite me. It's been a long day." He'd never known Trinity Frost to avoid a topic, making him all the more worried about what the man had to say.

"We caught the guy who shot up the lab." Eli knew Trinity wouldn't have missed his surprised expression, but he hadn't been able to temper his reaction. Trin gave him a small nod as if to say he understood. "He's a rent-a-thug who isn't known for being overly bright, but evidently he is smart enough to not give up the name of whoever hired him."

"Did he say anything that might implicate Cordesi?" Trinity shook his head, and Eli cursed under his breath before recounting his earlier conversation with the man they all suspected was responsible. Cordesi hadn't said anything self-incriminating, but Trin needed all the facts.

"He'll probably sit tight for a few days and wait for everyone to drop their guard before making any move. I can't see him waiting any longer—word on the street is the group he works for wants her brought in immediately." The scowl on the Sheriff's face made Eli think there was more to the story, but he knew it wouldn't do any good to push Trinity. Once the man made up his mind about something, there was little anyone could do to change it.

"Let me guess, they've tried tempting her with money and a new lab, but she hasn't taken the bait?" Trinity had probably nailed it. After hearing Evan wax poetic about London for the past year, it was a safe assumption.

"I doubt the loser we picked up knows, but if I was placing bets, that's where I'd put my money. She mentioned a consortium of big pharma companies, so I made a few calls. Everyone I've spoken to has acknowledged the group's existence, but they don't have or aren't willing to provide any other information." Eli didn't miss his friend's specific choice of words—he hadn't simply said those he contacted didn't know, rather he'd added they weren't willing to speak out about what Eli suspected was a powerful and motivated group of extremely wealthy individuals.

"Austin Adler is also investigating, and I suspect he'll enlist the Prairie Winds team as well." Trinity smiled because they both knew calling Kent and Kyle West was tantamount to pulling together the additional resources of Alex and Zach Lamont's ShadowDance team, Ian McGregor's elite group of computer specialists as well as the Morgans and Ledeks in Montana. Individually, each of them was a force to be reckoned with, but as a group, they were an unstoppable information gathering army.

"Keep me posted, and I'll do the same. Use the tunnels whenever you can, at least until we know what we're up against. No reason to advertise our movement." Trinity pushed out of his chair and took a couple of steps toward the door before turning back to Eli. "Although I don't know all the details of what Dr. Adler is working on, I'm damned glad there are scientists out there who are willing to put themselves at risk to help the rest of us. She's a brave woman."

Elijah couldn't have agreed more. Stepping forward, Eli shook Trinity's hand and thanked him for his help. "She's doing amazing work, and we'll do everything we can to make sure she can continue researching in a safe environment." He didn't mention one of the things Evan was already working on setting up a lab for London at the clinic. If Eli knew Evan, he'd stay up all night working to order state-of-the-art equipment—after he'd fucked London into a satisfied coma. There was room in one of the clinic's little-used wings for London to have a secure space to continue her work, and the two of them were not above bribing her with all the bells and whistles her little medical researcher's heart desired.

Once he was finally alone, Eli walked down the hall to the master suite. Stepping inside, he was pleased to see everything was already in place. He'd given the housekeeping staff precise instructions, and they'd gone above and beyond to make sure the space was perfect. Large bouquets of fresh flowers decorated the room, candles were set on tables and shelves waiting to be set aflame, and the enormous bathroom was filled with all London's favorite products.

During his search of her phone, Eli checked London's shopping history, making it easy to ensure the suite was filled with products he knew she loved. Immediate delivery hadn't been cheap, but she was worth the expense. The suite's small kitchen was well stocked with a variety of fruit and finger foods in anticipation of London's visit in a few hours. Before he returned to his own room, Eli checked both bedside tables and smiled when he found them well stocked with condoms, lube, and a nice selection of toys.

He closed the door on the large suite no one had used since he and Evan had it redecorated after his parents moved to a smaller cottage behind the main house. They'd laughed when their mom insisted the two of them work together on the remodel, insisting one day they would share the space and both needed to feel a connection to the larger than most luxury apartments. Julia Monroe could be a steamroller when she set her mind to something, and she'd also been adamant the new suite remain unused until they found their *one*. Neither Eli nor Evan had been able to imagine finding a woman to share, but now, their fathers' words replayed in his mind. *Listen to your mother, boys, I've never known her to be wrong about this sort of thing. She has always been able to see the future when it comes to affairs of the heart.*

Eli smiled when his gaze moved over the family portrait hanging over the mantle in the sitting room. The picture was a perfect representation of how all four of them viewed the woman who held all their hearts. Pausing before he took the last step into the hall, Eli backed up, switching the light on beside the picture so he could study it. He'd seen the portrait dozens of times and never noticed his mom was sitting to the side of the small settee. She wasn't sitting in the middle as expected. Instead, she sat on the half closest to his dads, leaving the half closest to her sons empty. Shaking his head, Eli turned off the small lamp before stepping out into the wide hallway and walking the short distance to his room.

Chapter Eight

L ONDON WASN'T SURE what woke her but felt a wave of panic begin to swell within her when she realized she was surrounded by darkness so complete, she couldn't make out her hand in front of her face. She sucked in a breath, trying to will her muscles to move, but it felt as if she was being held in place by a band of steel.

"Baby, I can hear your mind whirling so fast, you're going to make me dizzy."

A wave of relief swept over her as Evan's arm tightened, even more, pulling her back so firmly against his chest, she could feel the soft trail of hair brushing against her back and knew where it led. *Oh yeah, I know exactly where that happy trial ends…* At that moment, she felt the steel length of his very erect penis twitch against her ass.

"Feel what you do to me, London? The only thing keeping me from sinking myself into your slick heat is my worry you're too sore." She shifted a fraction and didn't notice any discomfort, but she doubted it would do her any good to argue.

"What time is it?" She was snuggled so deep in his bed surrounded by plush pillows, it was impossible to see the bedside clock.

"Are you still tired?" His simple question took her by surprise. London was so accustomed to living by the clock, she'd forgotten what it was like to listen to her body. "It's a simple question, baby. Don't give me the answer you think I want to hear or one you wish was true—just tell me how you feel. Anything less than complete disclosure is lying, London. I know how that brilliant mind of yours works, baby, and you already know enough about the lifestyle to understand how Doms deal with deception. Omission is still lying, and we won't allow you to lie to yourself either." She'd already admitted to researching the lifestyle, so it wouldn't do her any good to deny he was right.

His use of the word *we* wasn't lost on her, and she felt an involuntary shudder skitter up her spine. His vague references to his brother last night had faded under the intensity of their lovemaking, but the reality closed in around her now. "I want you to rest for another hour." London felt her body stiffen as she prepared to protest, but he turned her quickly, pulling her into his arms and giving her bare ass a sharp slap.

"You need to take better care of yourself, love. Resting is not a punishment. You know full well the benefits of sleep." He tightened his hold for several seconds before relaxing his arms, letting his hands move in slow, sensual circles over the globes of her ass. London's mind spun with questions. How could she have similar responses to a stinging slap and a warm caress? The books she'd read mentioned pleasure and pain being two sides of the same coin, but she'd assumed the words were nothing more than romantic fantasy… now she wasn't so sure.

"Fuck me, the scent of your sweet cream makes my

cock throb with desire." London's entire body responded to his every word. "I want to shove myself so deep inside your heat, you'll forget all about how tender those swollen tissues are." *Yes, yes, a thousand times yes... please... NOW!* His voice was little more than a growl, the animalistic sound setting aflame something inside her. When she squirmed against him, Evan groaned and moved back putting several inches between them.

"Please. I need you inside me." London barely recognized her own voice. The needy tone was one her mind associated with the women in the online videos she'd watched while researching dominance and submission. It was borderline terrifying to realize how needy she sounded.

Rolling her to her back, Evan moved her hands to the bed's elaborate wooden headboard and wrapped her fingers around one of the carved slats. "Hold on tight, baby. Don't let go. If your hands move, I'll stop, and you won't get the orgasm you're begging for. Do you understand?" She nodded, but he shook his head. "Words, London. You'll have to use words, so there is never any misunderstanding."

"Yes, I understand." By the time she uttered the words, Evan was already kissing a trail from her lips down the side of her neck, pausing to lick the pulse point behind her ear. His moan vibrated all the way to her pussy.

"You taste amazing, and feeling your blood pound against my tongue fills me with heat, baby." He continued the sensual assault, and by the time he reached her breasts, London was worried she was going to spontaneously combust. Sucking her puckered nipple into his mouth,

Evan rolled the sensitive tip with his tongue, and London let go of the headboard, threading her fingers in his hair. Her mind didn't register the movement until he released her nipple and raised a brow when her clouded vision cleared enough to meet his gaze. The dense fog of need finally cleared enough for her to realize what she'd done.

"I'm sorry, I was so caught up in the moment, I didn't realize I'd moved. I'm afraid I'm not very good at this whole... well, this... umm... sex thing."

"Sex thing?" The corners of his mouth twitched as they tipped up enough for her to see he was amused, and she felt her face flame with embarrassment. He slid back up to press a quick kiss against her lips, returning her hands to the headboard. "Trust me, love, you are very, very good at the *sex thing*. Now, keep your hands in place, or I'll bind them."

London was sure he'd intended the words as a pseudo-threat, but her body had an entirely different interpretation. Heat surged through her, the tendrils touching the most intimate reaches of her mind, making her moan as need swamped her.

"You are a gift straight from the Universe, and so fucking perfect, I can hardly wait to get you into the playroom and bind you."

London felt like she was sliding down a slippery slope toward release and wondered if he'd be able to make her orgasm with nothing more than words.

EVAN FOUGHT A smile as he watched London grip the

headboard so tightly, her fingers were turning white with the effort. As a shifter, he knew his saliva would go a long way to heal her traumatized tissues, but as a Dom, he knew how important it was to begin as he intended to go. If he let her get away with letting go when he'd specifically forbidden it, she wouldn't believe him the next time. Inconsistency would erode any relationship, but it would destroy the trust so essential between a Dom and his submissive before the relationship could even begin.

"Be a good girl and keep those pretty fingers where they belong, and I'll show you how sweet rewards can be. You've used up your one free pass, baby." He wanted London to begin making a positive connection between following his commands and pleasure. Evan might not be as strict as his brother, but he understood the importance of establishing a solid foundation for their D/s relationship. The better prepared she was, the easier it would be if she decided to commit to a polyamorous relationship.

"I promise to do my best, but when you touch me, my brain turns off."

He smiled at her admission and gave her a heated kiss as a reward for her transparency. The truth was, he wanted her brilliant mind to take a break and let her body lead for a while. He'd heard his friends at Club Isola talk about the joys and challenges of topping intelligent women and was grateful he'd paid attention. They were all experienced Doms, but they'd marveled at how rewarding it was to give their sub a much-needed break from the relentless chatter in their minds—they'd also bemoaned the challenges. He'd seen Abby Garrett run circles around her two Doms until they tied her to a St. Andrew's cross. There was something about being bound that allowed the little imp to fully let go, and Evan wondered if London's reaction would be the same.

"Don't let go, and I promise to make the effort worthwhile." Resuming his sensual assault, Evan used his mouth to map every delicious inch of her as he moved slowly toward his goal. Every nip of her sweet flesh was followed with a sweet kiss or soothing lap of his tongue. He watched her reactions and was thrilled when the sweet scent of her arousal floated around him. Moving his fingers to the junction of her thighs, Evan found the folds of her sex soaked with her cream.

Moving into position, Evan drew one long sweep from London's perineum to her clitoris. Feeling her shudder and hearing her shout his name had his wolf clawing for release. He felt his canines lengthen and forced the beast back before he lost the battle entirely. Circling the tiny bundle of nerves with the tip of his tongue, Evan relished the shrill cries filling the air around them as her body convulsed beneath his hold.

"You're such a good girl—keeping your hands exactly where they are supposed to be. Don't come yet, baby. Hold it off for a little bit longer, your release will be so much more powerful if you wait." Her look of disbelief made him grin. "I swear it will be worth the effort." He didn't expect her to be able to hold back her orgasm for long, she simply didn't have the experience required to hold the pleasure at bay for long.

"What? Seriously? Oh my God and Aunt Gerty, how am I supposed to do that?" Her voice rose a full octave before she stopped speaking, and Evan knew the perfect distraction. Pressing the tip of his finger against her anus, he felt her involuntary clench. "It's too much."

"You already know my brother and I want to share you, baby. You picked it up yesterday—Goddess knows you are too bright to have missed it. But are you brave enough to take a leap of faith toward what your heart desires, sweet London?" Her pussy gushed over his fingers, and Evan used her natural lubricant to ease his finger past the tight ring of her rear hole, pushing into the first knuckle.

"Sweetheart, your body answers for you. I know you were attracted to Elijah, and I suspect you feel guilty about it when you shouldn't. I was thrilled to see the sparks flying between the two of you." It was the truth. Knowing he and Eli might be able to follow in their parents' footsteps filled him with an overwhelming sense of hope for the future.

"I'm not supposed to want two men." She'd barely whispered the words, but he hadn't missed the tortured confession.

"Baby, let those Puritan restrictions go and listen to your body. We're going to see Eli in a few hours, and I can promise you he's going to have some very direct questions for you." His tongue lapped along the wet folds of her pussy, and Evan felt her begin to tremble. *Almost there, baby.* He was anxious to introduce London to their parents, but he wasn't about to bring up the topic of his mom and dads when he had his face buried between her legs. *Oh yeah, baby, the three of us are going to have a long chat about poly-relationships.*

"You taste like a Spring morning in the woods—fresh and filled with delicious anticipation of things to come." He swiveled his finger in her rear hole and smiled when she bore down, allowing him to edge in a second finger. Flattening his tongue over her clit, he pulled back just enough to give her the command to come before sucking the nub into his mouth. London's body reacted before he'd finished the words, her scream loud enough to be heard by whoever he'd heard puttering around in the kitchen several minutes ago.

The sweet syrup pulsing over his tongue made his cock throb, but he pushed thoughts of fucking her aside. He needed to let the healing properties of his saliva work their magic before he escorted London to his family home. They'd drive one of the golf carts in the tunnel, saving her energy for her time with Eli. Moving up to wrap her in his arms, Evan stifled a groan when she made a soft snuffling sound and pushed her lush ass against his cock. Her deep, even breathing let him know she was sound asleep, and he slowly moved out of the bed. Tucking blankets around her so she wouldn't miss his warmth, he watched her sleep for several minutes before slipping into his clothes and heading down the hall.

Evan wasn't sure who he'd been expecting, but the man leaning against the kitchen counter stirring a cup of steaming coffee hadn't even made the list. Cooper Hicks was dressed in a white button-down shirt, his long sleeves rolled up midway between his wrists and elbows. His faded jeans looked like they'd been washed one time too many, and his booted feet were crossed at the ankles. Evan knew, from his previous dealings with the former CIA operative, he was carrying at least one concealed weapon and likely three or four. The pose was casual, but there was an air of tightly coiled energy radiating from the man Evan knew was a friend of Ian McGregor's.

"I'm not going to bother asking how you got in, Cooper, but I am interested in why you're here." Evan didn't put much effort into hiding his annoyance—what the hell, it wouldn't do any damned good, anyway. The corners of Cooper's mouth twitched, and Evan wanted to roll his eyes. *I swear if he gives me any grief about London's screams of pleasure, I'll shoot him with his own gun.*

"Whatever you're thinking, you'd do well to reconsider, Evan. I'm not the enemy. Of course, if London was my sister, I might feel differently." Cooper paused for several seconds before nodding to the coffee pot, raising a brow in question.

Nice of him to offer me a cup of my own coffee. Abe and I are going to have a long chat about security.

After pouring his coffee, Evan moved to the other side of the counter, settling on one of the bar stools. Focusing his enhanced senses on the other man, he noted Cooper's measured breathing—obviously an effort to appear relaxed when he wasn't. The barely restrained energy shimmering around Cooper reminded Evan of heat waves he'd seen over sidewalks when he'd been in Arizona last summer. The dark tinge of color at the edges of Cooper's aura made him look more dangerous than he'd appeared the first time they met, but Evan sensed the other man's frustration wasn't directed toward him.

"London landed on the Agency's radar about a year ago. Her name kept popping up in dark web communication between members of a pharmaceutical consortium." He paused, and Evan got the impression *former* was not a term anyone should use to describe Cooper's association with his *former* employer. "I've kept track of the case because of my... *association* with Catalina."

Evan chuckled and shook his head. "Are the two of you still dancing around each other? I thought perhaps you'd moved beyond that pre-mating dance." The electricity arcing between Cooper Hicks and Catalina Adler had been intense enough to light up Broadway when the two of them had been at the clinic with Brooklyn. He'd had the sense the two had a history, but it didn't appear as though they'd been a couple.

"It's complicated." Cooper's terse answer might have deterred a nicer person, but Evan wasn't feeling particularly generous since Hicks had skirted several different levels of security systems before entering his private space. Shaking his head, Evan glared at Cooper.

"I need to check in with the clinic, so if you could cut to the chase, I'd appreciate it. Whatever brought you here is obviously significant, or you wouldn't have made the effort to waltz through my security."

Cooper smiled and set his empty coffee mug aside. "Your security is good, but it's not great. I'll help your team before I leave, then I'd suggest you have a long talk with Israel Adler. Security systems are his area of expertise, and he has a vested interest. From what I've heard, London is the brothers' favorite because she has never given them any trouble." Evan could only imagine how worried the Adlers were about their sweet sister, and until a few minutes ago, he'd have sworn she was in the safest place she could be. *Fucking hell.*

"Listen, I know you're unhappy I got past your security, but you're looking at it all wrong." When Evan raised a brow and tilted his head in question, Cooper sighed. "I really did come to help. The group trying to bring London onboard is done playing nice. They gave Cordesi more time than they planned, and for some reason, he's been stonewalling them. Just between us, I think he likes her—and it wasn't something he expected."

Evan had come to the same conclusion a few hours ago. Holding London in his arms while she'd slept, his mind had been too busy to nod off. With plenty of time to piece together the bits of information, he'd come to the same conclusion. Muttering a string of curses that would make his mother blush, Evan looked up to see Cooper grinning.

Letting out a deep sigh, Evan finally spoke. "It's easy to see why Cordesi would be attracted to her—she's fucking perfect. What I don't understand is why would he risk injuring her?" Shaking his head, he looked up to see Cooper studying him closely.

"Cordesi isn't an unknown to the Agency. We've seen him use charm to recruit for other groups, but this is the first time I've suspected he set up a scene to play hero."

"If the CIA was worried about London, why weren't they watching?"

"They were watching. How do you think I found out about this so quickly? It's not like it was on the fucking six o'clock news." Evan went utterly still at Cooper's words. He'd assumed London's family had asked Cooper to check on her, but he hadn't considered the man must have already been close.

"Catalina's been worried about London for some time.

She didn't like Cordesi, but she wasn't in a position to share any information with her sister." Evan looked at the other man and wondered at the shift in his tone when he realized Cooper was looking past him. Turning to see what had snagged Cooper's attention, Evan was surprised to see London standing at the edge of the kitchen, holding a white box tied with a sapphire blue ribbon. She was drowning in one of his white dress shirts, and he knew she had no idea how translucent the cotton fabric was in this light. Her hair was a mass of disarray, blonde curls tumbling around her shoulders, making her look like a sexy wood sprite. London Adler was so beautiful, she stole his breath.

Chapter Nine

L ONDON WOKE UP alone in Evan's large bed, and despite her best effort, hadn't been able to get back to sleep. Giving up, she pulled one of Evan's shirts from the large walk-in closet and slipped across the hall to the guest room to find something to wear. She'd been flabbergasted to discover the room empty except for her backpack and the box she held in her hand.

Moving down the hall in search of Evan, she was shocked to find Cooper Hicks standing in the kitchen. He'd nodded to her in greeting, but she'd quickly returned her attention to Evan.

"I'm sorry, I didn't mean to interrupt. I was wondering where my bags are?" Evan held out his hand, and her feet were moving before her mind registered the summons. Placing her hand in his, London felt a surge of warmth skitter up her arm, suddenly aware of how little she was wearing.

"I recognize that look, London, and you have nothing to be concerned about. As a Dom, I frequently see subs in a lot less."

She turned but could only stare blankly at the man she knew was interested in her sister. What did he mean *as a*

Dom? Holy shit, is Cat a submissive? She'd never considered the possibility, but then it had never occurred to her Brooklyn would turn out to be a submissive either.

"London, did you hear me?" Cooper's question caught her by surprise, bringing her back to the moment, making her realize while she'd been lost in thought about her sisters, he'd asked her a question.

"No. I'm sorry, I was thinking about my sisters. Having nine siblings and working in busy labs has taught me to tune out things around me." *Not to mention I'm more than a little inconscient because I'm standing here in Evan's shirt and nothing else in front of two men. One looks like he wants to eat me for lunch, and the other looks amused.*

"I asked when you last had contact with Franklin Cordesi." London fought the urge to roll her eyes… damn, did everyone and their dog know what an idiot she'd been? Wasn't it enough she felt like a fool for believing a man as suave and good looking as Franklin would be interested in her? Following close on the heels of London's feelings of frustration, knowing her personal failure was now common knowledge among a growing number of people was an overwhelming feeling of humiliation. She didn't realize tears were streaming down her cheeks until Evan growled at Cooper and pulled her into his arms.

"What the fuck, Hicks?"

"I simply asked when the last time Cordesi contacted her." Cooper pushed away from the counter where he'd been leaning, his long legs eating up the distance between them in a few short strides. "You remind me of my little sister, Lakyn. So smart you don't cope well with making what you consider a mistake. Let me assure you, sweetness, we all screw up from time to time, particularly in our personal lives. If you never make a mistake, you aren't living—and that would be the worst blunder of all." She nodded because she understood on an intellectual level, but her emotions were running rampant, and she wasn't entirely sure why.

Cooper looked to Evan as if seeking his permission for something, but London wasn't sure what. Evan gave an almost imperceptible nod and stepped back, putting enough distance between them to allow Cooper to step closer. Cooper's large hands cradled the sides of her face, his thumbs brushing over the damp tear tracks on her cheeks. Pulling her closer, he pressed a soft kiss against her forehead.

"I'm sorry if I hurt your feelings or embarrassed you. That was never my intention. Despite Lakyn's best efforts, I'm often brusque—although I'm sure Catalina would use a much more colorful and unflattering term."

London felt herself smiling at Cooper's admission because she had in fact heard Cat refer to Cooper Hicks by a variety of rude nicknames. London had teased her sister about their constant bickering being little more than foreplay and received Cat's middle finger salute in return.

"I'd like to help in any way I can. I'm already familiar with most of the aspects of what you've been facing, but I'd like to hear your side." Her surprise must have shown because he grinned. "Uncle Sam is a nosy old fart, London. He finds all sorts of reasons to poke his nose into your business. He likes to read your texts, emails, and listen in on your phone conversations."

"You've been spying on me?" London took an involuntary step back, stumbling over her own feet and would have gone to the floor if Evan hadn't caught her. Cooper shook his head.

"*Spying* has a very ugly connotation, I think *protecting* is more appropriate. Any time an American citizen's work puts them on the radar of world factions who don't necessarily have the same agenda as our dear Uncle, there are agencies assigned to make certain they aren't subjected to any *undue pressure*."

"Holy shit. That was the biggest bunch of PCBS I've heard in a long time... and you said it all with a straight face which makes it even more impressive." She knew her sister could spew Agency-based propaganda without batting an eye, but until this moment, London had never had the nonsense directed at her. Of all the reactions she might have anticipated, Cooper's bark of laughter wasn't one she would have expected.

"Damn, you are definitely Catalina's sister. Your voices are similar, but your language lacks a lot of Cat's more colorful curses. I guess I haven't been away from the Agency long enough to lose all the programmed responses." When she didn't respond, he shrugged. "Not to worry, Lakyn assures me working for the Wests means Tobi will set me on the straight and narrow in short order. To be honest, I'm not sure exactly what she means, but it doesn't sound good."

"I don't know Tobi West or Lakyn, so I can't comment, but I can assure you, the sales pitch won't work with me. I might have been naïve enough to believe Franklin Cordesi was attracted to me because I was an interesting companion and attractive enough to be seen with while out in public, but I'm not stupid." Before Evan's and Cooper's angry glares registered, London gasped as another piece of the puzzle fell into place.

"Did you send me the packet of information?" The look on his face was all the answer she needed, but she wasn't going to let him off the hook that easily. Narrowing her eyes and crossing her arms, she realized the movement lifted her breasts, pulling the shirt's fabric taut over her stiff nipples. *Dandy.*

"I didn't personally send it, no." Cooper was making a valiant effort to keep his eyes on hers. Evan, who'd moved to stand beside Cooper, wasn't even trying. *Insatiable much?*

"But you know who did." Her words had been more accusation than a question. "Fountains and fairy tales, this frosts my cookies. What time is it? Is it too early to start drinking? First, I have to fend off outrageous offers from numb nuts pharmaceutical executives who think everyone is as money hungry as they are… then they send their pretty boy to play footsie with me. Of course, I'm not smart enough to know when I am being played like an out of tune ukulele, so one of Uncle Sam's henchmen has to spell it out, complete with pictures of the man in question meeting with his employers." When Cooper flinched, she shook her head and rolled her eyes so far back, she should have seen her damned brain.

"Sadly, that's not the worst of it… I had to fire all my assistants and move into a hole-in-the-wall lab because I was so flipping paranoid. I changed my schedule every damned day to try to throw off the stalker I gained during this whole fiasco, and even that wasn't enough. It finally got bad enough, I packed up my minuscule piece of shit apartment, loading everything into my junker car, and the only place I could think of to park it was in front of the local Sheriff's office. Then some asshole shoots up the damned lab, sending me running into a freezing forest after they tried to slice and dice me with shards of glass. Now, I've involved the only man I've ever been truly attracted to and hot for his brother as well. Fucking fudge pops, I only decided to date Franklin because I thought I needed some experience before calling…"

"Stop." Evan's sharp command made her suck in a quick breath. As the enormity of everything she'd blurted out washed over her and she felt her face heat with mortification. Pointing at Cooper, Evan shook his head. "Your timing sucks. Didn't your super spook training teach you there are different interrogation methods for victims? If you have any more questions, they are going to have to wait until later. You've upset London enough for today— hell, enough for the next decade if you ask me." He'd muttered the last bit, but it had still been loud enough for London and Cooper to both hear. Turning his attention to her, he pointed the box she'd been carrying when she entered the room.

Holy cats, when did I set it on the counter?

"Make sure you read the card carefully and follow his instructions. I don't know how Eli managed to deliver it without me knowing he was here."

"How do you know it's from Eli? I'm scared it's anoth-er…" She hadn't planned to tell them about the packages she'd received. Damn it, why couldn't she learn to keep her mouth shut. She'd been terrified when she'd opened the first box and seen the pictures, but London was completely humiliated by the sex toys she'd received the next day. Cripes, she'd had to look up what a couple of the things were used for. *Who on earth wanted a glass plug with a tail shoved up their ass, anyway?*

"YOU'D BE SURPRISED, baby. There are all kinds of kinks. Now tell us about the other packages, then I want you to go back upstairs and take a long bath. I set out a variety of products, but if you don't find anything you like, let me know." When she stared at him blankly, he grinned. "I didn't read your mind, baby. You were speaking quietly but not quietly enough." She took a deep breath but couldn't seem to put her thoughts into words.

"Tell us about the pictures." The pads of two fingers were drawing slow circles over the pulse point on the inside of her wrist. She knew he was monitoring her reactions, but it didn't matter. His voice and touch were lulling her into a state of Zen calm she couldn't explain but appreciated it none the less. "You and I'll discuss the toys later." His expression changed to a wicked grin, and London let out the breath she hadn't realized she was holding. Relief swamped her as she realized how embarrassing it would have been to discuss anal beads and butt plugs with the man she knew her sister was interested in... even if Cat swore she had no interest in Cooper.

"I received a small box filled with pictures... all candid shots of me with various people. I assumed someone was sending a not-so-subtle message, wanting me to know they knew who was important to me and letting me know they had far greater access than I realized. It scared me at first, but it also made me more diligent." In her peripheral vision, she saw Cooper open his mouth to speak, but Evan shook his head as he held up his hand in the universal sign for *wait*.

"How was the box delivered? When did you get it, and where is it now?" Evan's eyes had turned molten with flecks of gold she had only seen dancing in his irises when he'd been making love to her.

"The box was delivered by a courier who'd been paid in cash by a woman whose description was so vague, it could be anyone. I got it two weeks ago, I remember because it was right after I'd gone to one of Cleveland's races. He'd called and invited me since he was racing at the South Boston Speedway. It's really rare for him to be racing so close to where I'm working, and I didn't want to miss the chance to spend time with him." She felt her voice catch and paused to take several deep breaths, trying to calm her nerves.

"There were a lot of pictures of the two of us... some of them were typical paparazzi shots—it had taken the reporters a while to find out I wasn't Cleveland's latest drive-by honey. But... there were also shots from the pre-race staging area, and the terrifying part was I didn't remember seeing anyone with a camera." She'd been completely stunned to realize how vulnerable she'd been. Whoever had been stalking her had gotten much too close.

"Why didn't you call me, baby?" Evan's voice held a note of sadness and disappointment she hadn't expected. She hadn't wanted to tell him about the pictures because the two photos that had terrified her the most were of the two of them. One had been during their argument about Evan sharing information about Brooklyn's condition. They'd gone toe-to-toe in the hall outside her sister's room, and London had been furious with him, but the pictures had shown something entirely different.

The photo was set against the darkened hallway with only the two of them softly illuminated by the light from the nurses' station behind her. Holy Hannah, the shot looked like it had been set up by a professional as a magazine-ready photo op. She'd been shocked to see how their body language defied what she knew was taking place at that moment. Her oldest sister, Asia, had been standing in the shadows and teased her that their battle of wills was little more than a primal mating dance. She'd been aghast at Asia's remark, but looking at the photograph as objectively as possible, London understood how her oldest sister might have misinterpreted.

Be honest with yourself, London. Asia saw what you hadn't been willing to admit, and her words have turned out to be as much prophecy as observation. And there you go talking to yourself again. Cripes, I'm losing my mind.

"I was scared." When his eyes darkened, she shook her head. "Not the kind of scared you are thinking. There were pictures of you and me at the clinic… and…"

"Pictures taken *in* the clinic? Taken *inside* my fucking clinic?" His voice had gone ice cold, and she attempted to take a step back, but he held her tight. "Stop. London, I'm not angry at you, baby, but I'm furious someone had the audacity to take photos inside my medical facility—I've worked my ass off to establish a safe haven for my patients—a hospital with a pristine reputation for privacy."

She could practically hear his mind spinning as he tried to put together a list of who had worked during that time.

London would bet she knew which nurse had taken the pictures, but before she could speak, she saw realization dawn in his expression.

"Carolee. If she hadn't already moved, I'd fire her this minute." He must have sensed London's unease because he studied her closely. "What did she say to you? And tell me about the pictures."

"She made it pretty clear the two of you were an item. To be honest, I didn't understand her insecurity until I saw the pictures." She ducked her head, trying to avoid looking him in the eye. Damn, there were moments when she was convinced Evan could see all the way into her soul, and in the few minutes she'd spent with Eli, it seemed he was as intense as his bother if not more so.

"Don't ever hide from me, London. I want all of you, baby, and that means I want to share everything—your fears and joy, insecurities, and triumphs. And I'm warning you now, Elijah is worse. He'll demand you are not only completely honest with us but honest with yourself as well." As a shiver of anticipation moved through her at the speed of light, heated desire spread rampantly in its wake. "I can't tell you how much that reaction pleases me, love." Letting his gaze flick to Cooper before returning to her, Evan smiled.

"If I had to guess, I'd say the pictures show the intense attraction between us. The heat we generated was enough to melt steel, and everybody knew this was inevitable." Pulling her into his arms, London felt the hard length of his cock pressing against her stomach. "Mine." His single word declaration whispered against the sensitive shell of her ear made her knees so weak, she wondered if they were knocking hard enough for the men to hear. "Where are the pictures, baby?"

"In my backpack." There was no reason to deny she still had them.

"You were trying to protect me, weren't you? That's why you didn't call anyone you care about when you knew you were in trouble, isn't it?" His words had been phrased as questions, but she knew he didn't really expect her to answer. When she nodded against his chest, London heard him sigh. "Never again, baby. From now on, Eli and I are the first people you call when you're in trouble, understood?"

"Yes, I understand, but I…"

"No. There is no *but*. This is non-negotiable, London. If you agree to try a poly-relationship, Eli and I will take our responsibilities very seriously—and chief among those will be your safety. The only thing that will ever trump our commitment to making you happy will be our lifelong pledge to your safekeeping." When she started to speak, he shook his head. "Non-negotiable." Turning her, he handed her the box, reminded her to call if she needed anything, and gave her ass a quick swat propelling her toward the stairs.

Before she could close the bedroom door, she heard Cooper's tight voice. "I want Carolee's full name."

"The pack will deal with her."

"I want her name and any information you have, Evan. I don't give a flying fuck what the pack does with her. We have some of the best techs in the world at our disposal, and we're damned well going to utilize them. It's important we know what her connection is to the Consortium. We don't know what lengths she'll go to in her efforts to keep the two of you apart."

Closing the door behind her, she didn't hear Evan's response and was grateful for the reprieve. The entire discussion had been an emotional roller coaster, and London had no illusions it was over. The more time she spent with Evan, the more casual his references to sharing her with his brother became, and she wasn't sure how she felt about that. Setting the box aside while she started the bath water, London wondered how Evan had known it was from Eli. Shrugging her shoulders, London could only assume he'd recognized the handwriting on the attached envelope.

Once the steaming water was streaming into the enormous marble bathtub London suspected had been designed for several people to share, she returned to the bedroom. Pulling the envelope from the top of the box, she carefully unfolded parchment paper, smiling when she saw the same flowing handwritten script.

I am counting the minutes until I see you again, sweet London. I'm looking forward to watching you walk through the door, wearing the gift enclosed and nothing else.

Elijah

Nothing else? Is he kidding? This box isn't large enough to hold an entire outfit. Sliding the satin ribbon from the box, London set the lid aside and unfolded the delicate, scalloped-edged tissue paper, revealing a perfectly folded piece of zaffre silk. The deep blue reminded her of the night sky in Alaska. Her parents had taken all ten of their children to see the Northern Lights, and while she'd enjoyed the dazzling display of color, it had been the haunting blue sky, preceding Mother Nature's bands of color, she'd always remembered. The dress would be obscenely short, and the narrow spaghetti straps would be the only thing keeping the dress from becoming a pool of silk around her feet. Her bare feet.

Digging frantically through the pearl colored tissue, London wondered where the rest of the outfit was hidden. Jumping when she heard a chuckle behind her, London spun around to find Evan leaning nonchalantly against the door frame. Her body responded to his in ways London had never anticipated, and for several seconds, she was rendered speechless. Holy hell he was so fucking hot, she could only gape at him with her mouth hanging open. He was deliciously tall, his muscular shoulders and chest and slender hips making him look like an Olympic swimmer. His sandy hair brushed the tops of his ears and curled over his collar, making him look just a bit unkempt, something she suspected was unusual for the man who was meticulous in his professional life.

"You keep looking at me like that, and we're never going to make it to the main house, baby." The heat in his gaze was a sharp contrast to the ice blue color of his eyes, and his second slow perusal was so intimate it felt like a physical touch. "I'll save you the trouble of searching—you won't find anything else in the box, love." He stepped forward, taking the dress from her clenched fist, holding it up by delicate straps which were little more than threads. "Eli has always had exquisite taste, but I must say, he's definitely outdone himself this time. The color is perfect—it matches the shade of your eyes right before you come. Eli is obviously anticipating seeing it for himself."

Chapter Ten

EVAN HAD KNOWN Eli was planning to send London a dress to wear today, but he hadn't expected his brother to be so bold in his choice. Hopefully, Elijah had managed to get two dresses—this one for their private meeting and something a bit more appropriate for London's introduction to their parents. Evan knew neither their dads nor their mom would be shocked, but London would be uncomfortable, and it was important she focused on the interaction between his parents rather than feeling exposed and vulnerable.

"It's a lovely dress… but it's too small." *Way too small. Miles too short and it's going to look like someone painted it on me.* Evan was surprised to hear the first echoes of telepathic communication building between them. He knew it was something most mates shared, but he hadn't expected it to begin until after they'd officially claimed her. "If I take a deep breath, I'm going to flash my pink bits."

"Pink bits?" Evan could feel the smile spreading over his face. "Baby, I don't think I've ever heard of a woman's pussy referred to as pink bits. I assure you, Eli knew exactly what he was doing when he bought this dress. Now, let's get you in the bathtub. You have an hour and a half before we need to leave. We'll be using the tunnel so you won't need a coat or shoes." *Or panties or a bra.* Grinning to himself, he shackled her dainty wrist with his hand and pulled her along behind him into the bathroom. He made short work of the buttons on the shirt she was wearing, then used the tip of his finger to draw a line from the hollow of her throat to her navel.

"I love seeing you in my shirt, but from now on, you're only allowed to button two buttons. I want visual and physical access to your body—*always*." Helping her into the steaming tub, Evan noticed she was biting her lower lip, the nervous gesture was one of her few *tells*. He held on to her arm when she would have settled into the water. "What's bothering you, London? And let me remind you, be honest—with yourself and with me."

"The whole *access thing* sounds a lot like exposure to me. I'm not sure I'm ready to be naked in front of other people. I mean... look at me."

"Oh, baby, I assure you I'm looking—and enjoying it immensely. Obviously, Eli is anxious to see the treasures you were hiding beneath the baggy clothes you seem to favor as well." Motioning for her to sit, he rolled up a small towel and held it in place until she'd settled back, resting with her head against the edge of the tub. "We'll get you a nice pillow, but this will do for now." He smoothed the loose tendrils of her hair back and smiled when he saw her nipples peak under his appreciative gaze.

"Open your legs, baby. I want your *pink bits* to get the maximum benefit from the healing properties of the bath salts." He saw her eyes trace to the citrus and sage product she'd chosen, and he grinned. "It wouldn't have mattered which scent you chose. I asked my housekeeper to get the same healing blend in a variety of fragrances." As a group, shifters were highly sexual creatures with little to no inhibitions, so he hadn't hesitated to make the request.

Growing up in an environment where people regularly shed their clothing before shifting negated any reluctance to being exposed or conversations others considered too intimate for anyone outside their immediate circle. From what he'd learned about the Adlers, the men hadn't made any effort to hide the fact they were shifters, but they hadn't shared any of the details with their sisters.

"Buying products for your dates' sore pussies is one of your housekeeper's duties?"

He heard the layers of questions beneath the snark and knew it was based in insecurity, but that didn't mean he intended to let her get away with it. Leveling a look at her, Evan cocked a brow, letting her know he didn't appreciate her tone. He saw her shift uncomfortably, but he continued to wait. He'd give her a chance to redeem herself by being transparent about what was really bothering her, or she was going to dig herself deeper. *I hope she chooses wisely.*

"How many women have been in…" Sighing, her shoulders dropping in what looked like resignation, she finally continued. "I guess it really isn't any of my business, but I hate thinking I'm just another notch in your bedpost."

Tipping her face up, so she was forced to meet his gaze, Evan kissed the tip of her nose. "Thank you for being honest, baby. It's much easier to resolve issues if we both know what we're dealing with." The next kiss slid subtly over her plump lips before he deepened it to the point, it held enough heat, he could practically feel his blood coursing through his veins. Evan knew if he didn't dial it back, she wasn't going to get the relaxing bath she deserved.

"I've never had a woman in my bed or in this bathroom, baby. There have been visitors in my home—family, friends, business associates—but none of them have ever been beyond the main part of the house."

"Thank you." London's shoulders eased back, and he was pleased when she visibly relaxed. "I know I didn't have any right to ask, but the question would have rolled around in my head like a snowball until it became a much bigger issue." Evan chuckled at the visual her words created. Standing up he stepped back and enjoyed the view between her slender legs for a long seconds before returning his gaze to hers.

"Thank you for trusting me enough to be honest. Communication is vital in every successful relationship, but it's even more important when dominance and submission are involved. Honesty and a willingness to try things that might well be out of your comfort zone will open up a whole new world for you, baby. All I'm asking is for you to keep an open mind."

London's nod was going to be answer enough this time because Evan could see her eyes glazing over as the events of the past few weeks started, once again, catch up with her. Evan felt his protective instincts surging to the surface and wondered if anyone had ever taken care of London in the way she deserved. He and Eli would care for her in every way, and he suspected protecting her from giving too much of herself would be one of their biggest challenges. They'd spend the rest of their lives making her the center of their family, just as their mother was the center of their fathers' lives.

"Relax for a bit. I have some calls to make before we go, so you have plenty of time." Evan wasn't sure she'd heard him since her eyes were already fluttering closed as he slipped out of the door. The tangy scent of blood tickled his nostrils, and he felt his senses sharpen as his eyes tracked to the bed. Gathering the bedding with the evidence of London's lost innocence, Evan smiled to himself, trying to shake off the primitive part of him yearning to howl in pride. He'd claimed her virginity, and he knew his brother was going to feel the same when he claimed her anally.

Evan had never seen his brother step completely from behind the iron curtain of control he kept firmly in place, but London was going to shred the professional distance Elijah always kept in place. The burden of taking over for their dads weighed heavily on Eli, and Evan often worried his brother would become so engrossed in his work, he would miss the opportunity to have a life. Hell, he'd nearly done the same thing before meeting London. *It's amazing what a difference the right person can make in your life.*

A little more than an hour later, Evan smiled when London asked about the towel on the passenger seat of the golf cart. Pack members used a variety of small, electric mobile transports in the tunnel, but he'd chosen the open-air car, knowing it would afford London a better view of her surroundings, and with a little luck, there would be enough of a breeze to enhance his view as well.

"I didn't want your bare cheeks and pussy chilled by the seat, baby." If he hadn't already suspected she'd defied

Elijah's order, he'd have known by her reaction to his response. Her eyes went impossibly wide, and the deep scarlet painting her cheeks was proof enough. Laughing to himself, Evan remembered the white lace thong she'd been wearing yesterday was missing from the clothes he gathered from his bedroom. He should have known she'd handwash the little scrap of nothing. She'd probably used the blow dryer for an extra thirty seconds to ensure the elastic and lace was dry—not that it was going to remain dry for long.

Pointing out safety features and escape doors along the way, Evan tried to keep London's mind occupied so she wouldn't worry unnecessarily about facing Eli. Of course, she'd complicated matters by wearing panties, but the punishment she'd earned wouldn't be anything she couldn't handle. With the end of the tunnel in sight, Evan hazarded a sideways glance and saw London fidgeting on the seat.

"Are you nervous, sweetheart or has the cool air kissing your bare pussy teased you into a state?" The guilt in her eyes assured him she would never get away with lying to them. *Perfect.*

"About that..." he knew she'd started to confess, but one of the tunnel managers stepped from the office before she could continue. Evan introduced her to Pete Neal before moving her quickly into the private elevator that would take them directly into the private family section of the house. Pete hadn't reacted to the practically sheer dress she was wearing, but it was only a matter of time before London realized how exposed she'd been in front of a complete stranger.

When the doors of the elevator slid closed, Evan heard what sounded like a whimper. His enhanced hearing would have picked up the sound a hundred yards out in a hurricane even if it had been barely audible, but this was so faint, he knew it had to have been little more than an echo in her mind. The telepathic link was continuing to strengthen, and he looked forward to the added information.

His bite would puncture her skin, transferring his DNA into her blood and small traces of her DNA into his bloodstream before he licked the wounds, healing them within seconds. She would reap a multitude of benefits from his shifter traits, and he would gain a soul-deep connection that would bind them together for the rest of their lives.

Evan and Eli would both be able to track London by scent over great distances. He hadn't been surprised his link to Eli was already growing stronger, but this development with London was so unexpected, he wasn't sure what to make of it.

We'll ask the dads. Just get our defiant little mate up here so I can paddle her pretty ass. Elijah's words filtered through his mind, and Evan bit the inside of his mouth to keep from smiling at the mixture of impatience and amusement he heard in Eli's voice.

Lowering the hand he'd pressed against her lower back, Evan caressed the rounded globe of her taut ass. He couldn't hold back his low chuckle when his fingers traced the narrow strip of elastic bisecting her cheeks, letting her know he was already aware she'd ignored Eli's command.

"Worried, baby?" He'd barely whispered the words

against her ear when the doors opened. Evan knew without looking his brother was waiting on the other side. London gasped and tried to take a step back, but Evan pushed her gently out of the elevator and into Eli's waiting arms. Eli wrapped her in his embrace after pulling her fully into the room.

"Princess, you look beautiful. I knew this dress would be perfect for you the minute I saw it. Come." Eli led her down the short hall to the kitchen, a move Evan hadn't expected. He'd assumed his brother would escort London into his office since it was much more private. Evan opened his mouth to ask, but the gleam in his brother's eyes was that of a cat who'd decided to play with the mouse before meting out the punishment she had coming, so he waited.

For many submissives, the anticipation of punishment and the gnawing guilt were a stronger deterrent than the punishment itself. Evan had been surprised to learn it was often the smartest and most successful women whose submissive nature ran the deepest. Their inherent need to please others might not reflect in their business dealings, but it was a shining beacon to the Dom they gifted with their trust.

Ian McGregor had once told him one of his biggest challenges with Callie was keeping others from taking advantage of her. The club owner had sworn his big-hearted wife and submissive would give until there was nothing left if he didn't intercede from time to time.

"Are you hungry, Princess?" They might have been standing in the kitchen, but you'd have to be a fool to think Eli was talking about food—and despite her naivety with

Cordesi, London Adler was no one's fool. The pink tinges on her cheeks let them know she'd heard the sexual undertone in Eli's question. Evan watched Eli's large hands caress London's arms in slow strokes, and his mouth watered when he saw her nipples draw up into tight points, reaching out for their attention.

"Could I have a drink, please?" She croaked out the words, and Evan knew she was struggling to make sense of the game Eli was playing. London's brilliant mind wouldn't miss the electricity arcing between the three of them, but she didn't have enough sexual experience to fully understand the dynamic. Keeping her off-balance would help them initiate her into their world, but it wouldn't see them through to the end. He and Eli were going to have to win her over quickly, or she'd feel obligated to leave once the problem with her stalker was resolved.

ELI STRUGGLED TO hold back his smile as he pulled their naughty sub from the elevator. He'd have known she was wearing a thong even if he hadn't heard Evan's laughter float through his thoughts when he settled her into the cart. He'd taken the small suitcases containing her clothes when he'd delivered the box, but it hadn't occurred to him to check his brother's bedroom. She was in for a big surprise when they got upstairs. There was a closet full of new clothes for her, but she was going to find very few lingerie sets. She wouldn't have many occasions to wear the offending garments—fuck it, if he had his way, he'd keep her naked as often as he could.

She was practically vibrating with the need to confess, and for the first time, Eli understood how his parents always knew when he and Evan had done something they weren't supposed to. Hell, who knew guilt had an entirely different energy signature? She'd asked for a drink, and he grinned at her disappointed look when he handed her a glass of water.

"I'll offer you something stronger after we talk. It's important you have all your wits about you during our chat." Her hand was trembling as she took a sip of the water, but she didn't respond. "I know Evan has told you a little bit about what we're looking for, so let's start by giving you the opportunity to ask questions." He hoped his part of the explanation could be covered by her questions—if she was brave enough to ask them.

He was glad he'd been watching her closely, or he might have missed the subtle shift. Evidently, he'd pushed the right button because he saw Dr. London Adler, the gifted academic and researcher, emerge right before his eyes. *Questions are what our mate does best, brother. You've stepped into it now.* Evan's words moved through Eli. He was equally shocked and pleased at how quickly their telepathic link was growing. London set her glass on the counter and straightened her shoulders—concern about the thong she was wearing pushed to the back burner for the moment.

"Evan has spoken about a polyamorous relationship, but I don't know how that could work long-term. It's not legal to have more than one husband. I'm not saying you're asking me to marry you or anything, but I don't want to start something then find out down the road a long-term union was always unattainable. I don't think my heart could take falling in love, then losing one or both of you. I know there are people in the kink community who claim to have ménage marriages, but I've never had any reason to interview them." She stopped to suck in several deep breaths, making Eli wonder if the move was motivated by a need to collect her thoughts or a need for oxygen. Holy Mother Goddess, how had she managed to blurt out so much without stopping to take a breath.

"Geez, listen to me. I'm thinking like a researcher instead of a woman who is currently up to her ass in alligators on multiple levels. I was dumb enough to think the one man who feigned interest in me could teach me enough about sex, I'd be desirable to the man I was really interested in and launched myself into the twilight zone. I'll probably have to return my Mensa membership card and decoder ring." Holding back a bark of laughter was all Eli could manage, keeping the grin from curving his lips had been impossible—thank Goddess his mate was too distracted to notice.

London was pacing the length of the kitchen, bare feet silent on the marble floor. Each time she passed in front of him, Eli fought the urge to pull her into his arms, but he knew she needed to work this through in her own time. Looking to Evan, he saw the corners of his mouth twitch as he mouthed the words *needs focus*. Eli agreed, and he'd love nothing more than to bend her over his knee and warm her backside. It would probably help her focus, but if she wasn't ready, it could very well end this before they ever got started.

Elijah and Evan were both sexual Dominants, but Evan

had always been more drawn to the social aspects of the lifestyle. Evan's Club Isola membership was his way of connecting with other like-minded individuals, but Eli had never felt the same need. He preferred his private play-room—his willingness to share extending only to his brother. Evan realized his need for privacy was even more profound now that London was starring in all his fantasies. The next time she stormed by him, muttering about how out of control her life was spiraling, he snagged her wrist, pulling her quickly against him.

"I hear a lot of observations but very few questions, so I'm going to help. First and foremost, we have many friends and family members in poly-relationships. Having been raised where this type of relationship is not only common but coveted, I'm sure we're ahead of you in understanding how it works. We'll encourage you to ask questions as long as they are respectful." When she gave a short nod indicating she understood, he slid his fingers under her hair to cradle the back of her neck with his large hand.

We have to be very careful with her, brother. She is like a forest sprite, delicate and petite. Evan's concern was real, and Eli agreed their size difference was a concern. The last thing he wanted to do was hurt her.

It will be hard to remember because her sharp mind makes her seem almost larger than life.

And there is a very large personality lurking beneath the sur-face—you've only gotten a fleeting glimpse.

Eli could hear the amusement in his brother's voice and vowed the two of them needed to have a serious conversation about London as soon as possible. If they wanted to be successful, they would work out any challenges out of London's presence. Their mom had always sworn the success of their unconventional marriage was primarily due to her husbands' commitment to working out any issues of jealousy or disagreements without involving her.

"Tell me how the sex part works." London's words took him by surprise, and Elijah found himself smiling down at her. Standing this close emphasized the difference in their heights, and Eli's mind flashed to how much he was going to enjoy finding ways to compensate for the discrepancy. When he didn't answer her immediately, London started to fidget with nervous energy.

"Too blunt? I actually hear that a lot, you know. Sometimes, things dart out of my mouth without checking in with my brain. Damn. Sorry. Listen, why don't we try this again tomorrow. Maybe I need to take a little time to think about all this first. I'll do better if I have a chance to make an outline that prioritizes my concerns."

What the fuck? No, sweetheart, tomorrow isn't an option. Eli may have just met London, but he knew women and didn't doubt for a minute if he let her walk away, she'd find a reason to run, and they'd never see her again. It would only take one phone call to any of her brothers before she was whisked out of their care—probably within the hour. Shifters mated for life, and they recognized their *one* quicker than non-shifters—meaning the few minutes he'd spent with London solidified his belief she belonged to him and his brother.

"We'll take you together and separately, Princess. You'll find shifters are highly sexual. We're also fiercely loyal and protective." Eli knew he'd only given her a partial answer, but he'd seen Evan step forward and wanted to ensure they worked together to provide the answers to her questions.

"You'll never be expected to keep track of who's turn it is, nor do we want you to feel obligated to keep things balanced. If you want to spend time alone with Eli, I'll respect that." Evan's gentle reassurance loosened some of the tension Eli felt vibrating through her.

"And I'll do the same." Eli nodded in agreement before Evan continued.

"Eli and I have spent our entire lives watching how our dads handle things with Mom. I'm not saying it was always smooth sailing, but I can tell you their love and commitment to each other always prevailed."

Eli studied London's expression and body language as Evan spoke. She focused on Evan's face, but he would bet her mind was processing the words as quickly as they were spoken. The small wrinkle between her brows indicated she was concentrating, but her pulse had picked up at the base of her throat, and her breathing was becoming shallow. *Damn you have to love a responsive woman.*

"Keeping track of my own schedule is enough for me, I wouldn't want to be responsible for anyone else's. I was actually asking about the logistics of being with two men at the same time. Does it really work like the books say? I thought about watching videos, but my internet has always been through the lab, and it didn't seem smart to have that on my browser history." Her eyes widened, and she gasped, causing him to grip her arms.

"What's wrong, Princess?"

"Holy shit. I don't have a lab to work in. How could I have forgotten about that? How am I going to find another lab? Dancing dust bunnies, I'm going to have to call Austin. Damn. He'll drop a net over me until Israel gives me the all clear, and God only knows how long that will take. I'll probably be old and gray by the time I get out from under their thumbs. Do you have any idea how crazy they are about this stuff?"

Eli shot Evan a glare when he snorted back a laugh.

Yeah, sweetheart... I know all about possessive and overly protective, and your brothers will have nothing on the two of us.

Chapter Eleven

L ONDON KNEW EVAN and Elijah were communicating, but she wasn't sure how. The air between them was nearly crackling with the power zinging back and forth. She'd seen her brothers do something similar but honestly, hadn't paid much attention. Now, the scientist in her wondered if true telepathic communication was possible, leaving the woman standing between them out of the loop. *Maybe I can learn to tap into their silent chit-chat. Bet that would be damned enlightening.*

The kitchen Eli had led her to when she'd first arrived was so large, she'd wondered for a minute if they had an onsite restaurant. When they'd first entered the space, Evan must have seen her surprise because he'd leaned close and whispered a quick explanation against her ear. Evidently, this part of their home served as the hub for the entire pack, and most of their meals were eaten together as a group. He explained there was a smaller kitchen in their private suite of rooms, and she was starting to think she might need a map.

London's brain-rattling realization she didn't have a lab to work in felt like running head-first into a brick wall. What the hell was she going to do? She didn't want to leave, but she didn't see any other option... her work was too important to simply set it aside while she played slap and tickle with the Monroe brothers.

"This sucks big blue monkey balls. Just because I don't want a bunch of big pharma jerk-offs getting their hands on my research, I'm going to be stuck dealing with my brothers. Damn and double damn, I finally get a chance to... well, to..." *Craptastic.* She'd started talking without thinking through what she was going to reveal—*again.* She hadn't dated in high school, and she'd rarely gone out, even with a group, during college. The older she got, the more glaringly her inexperience showed.

Chewing on her lower lip and studying the floor as if it was the most interesting thing she'd ever seen, London wished she'd listened more to her sorority sisters chatter about their boyfriends and dates. At the time, it had seemed unimportant, but now, she could see how valuable it would be to know when to blurt out her feelings and when to play her hand closer to her chest.

"I'd love to know what she's thinking." She started at the sound of Evan's voice. When had he moved so close? He was standing shoulder-to-shoulder with Eli, the two of them watching her, mild amusement lighting their eyes.

"If she's worried about a place to work, perhaps you should tell her how you spent a good portion of your morning." Eli might have been speaking to Evan, but his eyes never left hers. "Dr. Monroe has been busy, Princess. His clinic was designed to accommodate what we all hope will be a growing pack population, so there are areas of the facility that aren't currently being utilized."

Evan's smile made her breath catch. The man was

movie star gorgeous—and it always caught her by surprise. Amazingly, she seemed to have a similar reaction to Eli and wondered if their effect on her would always be this primal. Watching Evan's ice-blue eyes as they studied her in return, she found her body responding as his pupils darkened several shades as he became aroused. His eyes were framed by the longest eyelashes she'd ever seen on anyone, making him look innocent and sexy at the same time. Looking from Evan to Eli, London was struck by how much they looked alike with one significant difference—Eli's eyes were a brilliant shade of green.

The corners of Eli's mouth twitched in something close to but not quite a smile. "She's wasting a lot of energy worrying about her brothers—energy we could be putting to better use, Evan."

"I agree, but damned if I've found a way to keep her mind centered on what I've been trying to explain. Our bright little mate can't seem to remain focused. I'd love to tell her about all the cutting-edge equipment we've ordered for her new lab, but I think maybe we need to help narrow her focus a bit first."

"The orgasm you gave her yesterday before she met with the security team seemed to have a positive effect on her ability to stay on topic, but I'm not sure she's earned that reward."

The knowing glint in Eli's eyes told her he already knew she'd worn more than he'd given her. She knew Evan had figured it out, but she wasn't sure how Eli had known since he hadn't touched her other than a hug and stroking his warm palms up and down her arms. She leaned back against the hand cradling the back of her neck and sighed when his fingers gently massaged the tense muscles. London felt herself melting into Eli's touch, her eyes closed as a soft moan slipped past her lips.

"Oh… that feels so good. I think you have magic fingers."

"You have no idea, Princess. They'll bring you so much pleasure, you'll think you're coming apart at the seams, but there are rules, love." Eli's voice was reeling her in. She wasn't sure what had changed, but something in his tone was different. Melodic. Hypnotic. Compelling. "You're a good girl, and I know you understand the concept of rules, London. What were my instructions, Princess?"

London felt herself begin to surface from the haze surrounding her, but his fingers gripped her tighter, massaging the knotted muscles in her neck as his warm breath wafted over the sensitive shell of her ear.

"Instructions, London. What were they?" She repeated the note to him verbatim and felt him smile against the dewy skin along the side of her neck. *Geez, when did it get so warm in here?* "Did you follow my instructions, Princess?"

"I couldn't leave without panties. It's just not done. I thought you forgot them even though Evan said you didn't include them on purpose." She moaned as the pads of his fingers pressed against a particularly sensitive spot. *Much more of this and I'm was going to melt into the floor.*

"I won't make mistakes with your clothing, sweet girl. You should have listened to Evan, it would have saved you a spanking." London wasn't so far under his influence she didn't register the words, but her body had gone completely rogue, heating in all the places it shouldn't in response to his comment. "I can smell your desire, love. I'm not sure a spanking is going to be much of a deterrent, but I'm going to enjoy finding out." Before she knew what was happening, he'd turned her to face the largest commercial-grade refrigerator she'd ever seen. Her feet were spread wider than was comfortable, but not far enough she was in danger of falling. "Lean forward and hold on to the handles, London."

The air around her shifted, and she felt a warm hand cup her jaw so gently, it was closer to a caress than a move intended to hold her in place, preventing her from turning her face to the side. London's eyes met Evan's, and she could have sworn she could feel his concern.

"You said you've been reading about dominance and submission, baby, so I'm sure you have heard about safe words. We'll be using the stop light system. Tell me what that means to you."

"You'll ask me a color, and I'm expected to respond with one of the three colors on traditional traffic lights. Green means I'm okay to continue. Red means I'm past my limit, either physically or emotionally."

Her muscles were already beginning to tremble from the strain of her position, and she made a mental note to get back into the gym. The past year had been a never-ending schedule filled with little more than work. She'd stopped going to the yoga classes she loved and given up her trips to the gym because there never seemed to be enough time to find one she liked before she'd been forced to move on. When she'd been forced to let all her lab assistants go because the information had been leaking about her project, she'd given up anything resembling outside distraction.

When she'd been a young girl, London had made the mistake of telling one of her friends about her infatuation with one of the boys in their class. The next day, she'd been greeted by the jeers of her fellow students, and she'd left school that day sadder but wiser. Later, her mom had wiped away her tears and cautioned her the only way to keep a secret was to not tell anyone else. It was a piece of advice London decided could be applied in a wide variety of circumstances, and she'd played her cards close to her chest ever since.

Laughter behind her brought her back to the moment. Blinking, she refocused on Evan's concerned face, but the man speaking was standing behind her.

"I don't think I've ever seen anyone take a mental road trip in the middle of an explanation about safe words, brother."

"She's adrift. We've got our work cut out for us, but the reward is going to be worth every moment of the challenge." Using his thumb, Evan stroked over her cheek and smiled. "Finish it baby and stay with us. You aren't going to need a safe word for this punishment, but since this is a first between us, we want to make certain you know the power is yours. Our dominance depends on your submission, London. We will never take anything from you that is not freely given."

"Yellow means I've got questions, or I need a break." She wasn't sure why her mind was so scattered, but Evan's description of her as adrift was as accurate as anything she could come up with. She'd been burning the candle at both ends for so long, she had forgotten what it was like to have downtime, and the worst part was… she knew better. Not giving her mind a chance to reset had always led her into trouble.

A warm palm smoothed over her bare ass, and London realized, at some point, Eli had moved the back of her dress up to her waist. The caress was sensual enough to tempt her into believing this was how Eli intended to punish her for wearing panties, but London instinctively knew there was more to come.

"Your ass is amazing, Princess. Creamy skin covering perfectly rounded cheeks that are firm but not so rock hard they won't jiggle when slapped."

She felt herself stiffen. Jiggle? Holy shit! She had to find a damned gym as soon as this stalker nonsense was over. The first slap to her ass caught her off guard. She yelped and tried to stand up, but a firm hand spread between her shoulder blades keeping her in place.

"You are wrong, London. We don't want a mate who is rock hard. Your curves are amazing. And I'm warning you now, if you try to diet or exercise them away, you'll find yourself answering to both of us."

Evan's words brought tears to her eyes—she'd always felt like the ugly duckling in her family. Damned if her brothers and sisters weren't so beautiful, they'd been known to stop traffic.

"Don't you dare drift away, London. Let Eli help you focus, you'll be amazed how much better you're going to feel after you let all those worries dissolve around you."

The sound of lace tearing made her cringe. "Damn it, I loved that thong, and all of my other clothes have disappeared. I swear Evan's house is haunted… stuff mysteriously appears, then disappears just as quickly." This time both men chuckled.

"Baby, my home isn't haunted, but we may need to change some of the locks. Trin brought the clothes in, and Eli took them back out. Unfortunately for you, he didn't think to look in the bedroom which left you with the temptation to wear something you weren't supposed to."

"Sounds like a lot of traffic to me. Maybe that's where you need the damned stop light." The swat that followed her whispered response was much sharper than the previous one, making her whimper.

"Careful, Princess. We won't talk to you disrespectful-ly, and we expect the same consideration from you. Teasing has its place, but I assure you, snark during a punishment scene is never going to be in your best inter-est."

Looking down where the tattered remnant of her pant-ies lay on the gleaming wood floor, London bit the inside of her mouth to keep from responding. She had enough experience with dominant men to know they were rarely interested in discussing anything, they only cared about obedience. Explanations were seen as excuses and quickly dismissed.

Asshats, they say they want open communication, but it looks like the two of them only want me to talk when I'm giving them information they'll be able to use against me, or if I'm kissing their hotter than hell backsides and agreeing with them.

ELI WATCHED LONDON intently, focused on her every breath and movement as he gave her the swats she'd earned when she put on that damned breath-stealing scrap of lace. He spread the strikes out over her delectable bottom, making sure he gradually increased the intensity without ever reaching the point where he would have started with more experienced subs. She might think he only wanted compliance, but nothing could be further from the truth.

London Adler's spirit was continually battered by her insecurities. Instead of seeing her own brilliance and beauty, she compared herself to her siblings and felt as though she was lacking. *It boggles the mind.* Eli seriously doubted any of her siblings knew how she felt. Austin Adler didn't seem like the type to stand idly by as his sister's heart ached when he had the power to fix it. He and Evan would spend the rest of their lives making sure London understood her true worth—and her value had nothing to do with her groundbreaking work in the lab either.

Eli pressed his palm over the scarlet imprints left by his hand. The move would intensify the heat London felt and push her closer to the catharsis he knew she needed. Their sweet mate did not know how bottled up her emotions were, but he and Evan both knew the damn needed to be breached before the stress further affected her health. Letting his nostrils flare when the sweet scent of her arousal swirled around him, Eli fought the urge to claim her here and now.

You're not fucking her in the middle of the common kitchen, brother—at least not yet.

Eli could hear the amusement in Evan's voice and sent up a silent prayer of thanks for their enhanced telepathic link. Their dads had told them to expect the power of silent communication to grow, but he'd underestimated how significant the difference would be.

"Push her a bit more, she needs to vent some of the emotion swirling around in that brilliant mind of hers."

Reaching under her, Eli slid his other hand from her abdomen up to cup her breast, then pinched her tightly puckered nipple and held it tightly between his fingers while he rained down another series of swats. These slaps weren't as harsh as the others, but having them fall without any time for recovery, along with the sharp pinch of her nipple was enough to tip the scales.

London screamed as her knees folded, her orgasm blasting through her without warning. He caught her easily with one arm and held her in position until the final shudders of release faded, leaving behind the raw emotion so many submissives experienced after a particularly intense session. New subs experienced what many described as having the rug yanked out from under them— there was often a backlog of negative emotion they needed to purge before moving on.

Eli felt the moment everything shifted from sated bliss to emotional turmoil, and it felt like a punch to the gut hearing her heart-wrenching sobs. Lifting her into his arms, he moved to their private portion of the house, grateful no one else had entered the common area during the short scene. He'd wanted to purge the negativity swirling around London, but that didn't include embarrassing her in front of people he hoped would soon be a part of her daily life.

Sitting in front of the fireplace, Eli settled her flaming backside on his lap and bit back a smile when she hissed. The abraded skin would fare a lot better against his bare leg, but he didn't want her to send her screaming if she wasn't ready for them to proceed. Eli grinned when his link with Evan crackled with a plethora of derisive remarks about his overinflated ego. Eli was only egotistical because he knew how much the trait annoyed Evan, and like most brothers, annoying one another was one of their favorite sports.

Evan knelt in front of them to tuck a soft throw around London as her racking sobs finally started to abate. "You did beautifully, baby. I'm so proud of you." Eli watched her eyes flutter open, their blue depths swimming in leftover tears. She looked at Evan as if she wasn't sure he was sincere. "We won't ever lie to you, London. There may be times we tell you something doesn't concern you and refuse to answer questions, but we won't lie."

"If we're planning something special for you, we might very well simply ignore your inquiries, but we won't lie, Princess. It will take time for you to trust us, and we'll always honor the gift by being completely honest." Eli struggled to stifle a growl when London tried to shift into a more comfortable position which also moved her sweet ass over his rigid length. Having her lush derrière pressed against his cock was one thing—grinding her heated flesh over his throbbing erection was something else entirely. When she moved a second time, he tightened his hold and groaned. Evan chuckled and leaned close.

"You'd better sit still, baby. Eli seems to be holding on by a thread, and we still have guests to greet downstairs."

"Guests?" She struggled to get off Eli's lap—he was shocked at how difficult their petite mate was to contain. *Holy hell, she's all like a damned spider monkey—all arms, legs, and determined energy.*

Determined to hold her in place without adding any more sting to her already scarlet derrière, Eli elected to distract rather than scold her. Leaning her back against his arm, Eli pressed his lips to hers and slipped his tongue between them when she gasped in surprise. What was supposed to be a quick kiss to redirect London's worry about their company quickly morphed into something much more intense, making it infinitely harder to pull back.

"Last night, I dreamed of kissing you, but reality turned out to be even better. You taste like the spun sugar treats we used to get at the fair when we were kids." Eli could easily be addicted to kissing his sweet London. Damn, she was testing his resolve to be sure she was ready for everything he'd planned.

"We didn't get treats when we went on outings. It was too expensive to buy ten of anything." London's voice held a hidden longing and a child's disappointment at being denied the small surprises and indulgences most children enjoy. Eli's eyes cut to Evan's, his brother's expression confirming he'd heard it as well. It was easy to forget London's humble beginnings because her brother had done such a remarkable job of turning the business around after her parents died. Austin Adler's success was nothing short of spectacular.

"Next summer, we'll take you to the fair and let you have all the sugary delicacies you want, baby." Evan was still kneeling in front of them, and Eli wondered if London realized his brother had taken her small hands in his. Eli had slipped his free hand through the folds of the throw they'd wrapped around her and pressed his palm against her stomach, smiling to himself when he realized if he spread his fingers, his touch would reach from the lower curve of her breast to the top of her slit.

London's eyes dilated—until there was nothing more than a narrow ring of blue surrounding her pupils—when he let the tip of his finger slip into her wet heat. The band of color matched many of the things he'd bought her to wear. Her eyes were becoming unfocused, splotches of red marring her cream-colored skin still remained. The mottled red left behind by her crying was fading as the flush of arousal spread up from her chest. Every stuttered breath was a siren's call to his wolf, the combination of the fear of the unknown and blazing desire was sending all the blood from his brain to his cock.

"Lay back, Princess. We're going to play with you a bit before we go downstairs. Let's see if we can't map a few of the spots that make you sizzle. Evan and I want to taste you." Eli watched her eyes widen as she started to relax back into his hold. He'd positioned himself so she would be able to recline against the arm of the sofa, putting her in the perfect position for them to have a perfect view of her pussy. London's back no sooner touched the padded arm than she sat back up, glancing quickly from him to Evan, locking on him.

"But I want to taste you, too. Both of you." The flush painting her cheeks deepened with embarrassment, and Eli felt his cock twitch. In his mind's eye, his cock was slipping into the warm recesses of her mouth, his imagination kicking into high gear when she unconsciously licked her lips.

"Bed. Now."

Chapter Twelve

E VAN KNEW HIS brother had planned to wait to make love to the woman they already considered theirs, but there had been no way for him to deny her when she'd whispered her desire to taste them. They'd simply planned to savor her, but both understood how her tender heart would be hurt if Eli rebuffed her. Evan could feel Eli's internal struggle—as the stricter of the two of them, Elijah was protocol driven when it came to subs.

Most Dominants would have seen her request as topping from the bottom, but Evan was sure that wasn't the case with London. Hell, she didn't have enough experience to make demands of any kind—her request had come from her need to please them and her insatiable desire to learn.

Stripping while Eli settled London on the enormous bed, Evan smiled when he saw her looking at how much space surrounded her.

"This bed is huge. Where on earth did you find it and don't you get lost sleeping here by yourself?" London's face blazed as soon as the words slipped by her plush lips. "Oh damn, I'm sorry, that was very presumptuous, wasn't it? Of course, a man as good looking as you are doesn't sleep alone. Wait. Maybe you have another room for liaisons like

Evan?"

What the hell? Where did she get such a crazy idea?

His brother's bark of laughter broke the spell, or who knows how long Evan might have stared at her blinking in confusion.

"Princess, I assure you neither of us has brought a woman into our private domain. We both saved this master bedroom, hoping the Universe would send us a mate to share." Eli finished undressing before moving slowly onto the bed, positioning himself at London's feet. "Open those lovely legs for me, Princess. I want to enjoy the view while we continue this conversation." When she hesitated, Eli's eyes narrowed. "The only acceptable answer is, *Yes, Sir.*" London nodded quickly, but her legs opened much slower than either of them would find acceptable once she learned the rules.

"Yes, Sir." Her response was hesitant as her eyes flickered from his erect cock to his brothers. "I don't think… well, in the books I read, they talked about double penetration, and I really don't think that's possible with you. I mean… you seem… well, I'm no expert, but I suspect you are larger than most men and—" Evan moved to her side, smiling as he pressed his fingers to her lips.

"While this conversation is good for our egos, it isn't good for you to worry about something we plan to take care of, baby." He'd found her clinical description of what she'd read in romance novels amusing, but it didn't surprise him she would cut to the chase. *Always a scientist at heart.* "I'm a physician, London, do you really believe I'm not fully cognizant of what your petite body can accommodate?" He watched her tension fade and let his eyes move over her. "Damn, you are amazing, baby. Creamy skin we can't wait to lick and curves in all the right places."

"Will you show me how you like to be sucked?" Evan felt his eyes widen at her question, and Eli hadn't made any effort to cover his snort of laughter.

"Oh, Princess, I assure you, we'll help you master the skill—no matter how much practice it takes." Eli's grin was feral, but Evan doubted she'd seen it because her eyes were focused on his erection.

"Practice? Oh geez, I was hoping it would be something that sort of came naturally. Shoot, I probably should have watched those videos after all."

You're an ass, Elijah. Evan couldn't believe she'd taken his brother seriously. Didn't anyone in her family ever joke about anything? Eli's eyes reflected his surprise as well, but he didn't respond. Instead, he moved into position, lowering himself until his face was inches from her sex.

I'll make it up to her, you'll see. Eli's tone had been teasing until the first swipe of his tongue through her silken folds. *Fuck me, she tastes fantastic. You should have warned me. We may miss the company I can hear gathering downstairs.* The first swipe of his tongue through her folds had her arching off the bed with surprising strength.

Eli pressed his hands against the tops of her thighs, forcing her back to the surface, growling in warning. The fingers Evan had been using to roll her nipples into tight peaks was now resting across her upper torso, or she might well have levitated off the fucking bed. Eli slipped his middle finger inside her slick heat and smiled.

"You're soaking wet, Princess and so beautifully responsive, my control is hanging by a fraying thread." Eli's pleasure pulsed through Evan as if it had been his own when a fresh wave of her sweet cream moved over his tongue in response to his words. Hell, someday Evan wanted to find out if he could make her come with words alone—but not today. Today he wanted to watch as his brother tasted their mate for the first time. Eli opened his mind, and Evan could feel her vaginal walls clench around his tongue and fingers. His cock throbbed in response, and he moved into position. Today, he wanted to show her how much pleasure she could find in submission.

"Open up, baby. I've been dreaming of this moment far too long." Evan watched his cock slip between London's lips and chuckled when his brother muttered a string of curses as his control was tested.

Evan had spent a lot more time with London, so their connection was stronger. Eli was looking forward to spending time alone with her and knew he needed to do so before her lab equipment arrived in a few days. He might not know London well, but he knew enough to see she would immerse herself in setting up the lab and resume her work, which meant her free time would be limited.

We'll make certain she paces herself, brother. Evan's voice drifted through Eli's mind, interrupting his wayward thoughts. *For now, you need to focus on getting our little sub off, so her body is ready for you—and for Goddess sake, hurry up.* Eli laughed to himself when he heard his brother's desperate demand—apparently, London was a quick study when it came to blow jobs. Flicking his tongue over her clit, Eli marveled at the sensitivity of the tiny bundle of nerves.

"Look at this ripe little berry—bright red, sweet as sugar, and waiting so patiently for my attention." He sucked the pretty little button between his lips and felt her stiffen beneath his hands as her strangled scream filled the room.

"Baby, I'm going to come. If you don't want me to come down your throat, you need to let go. *Now!*" Evan's voice sounded strained even to his own ears, so Eli had to know how torn apart he felt. A part of Evan wanted to give London a choice because he knew how inexperienced she was, but the beast within wanted to know he'd marked her, and she'd be carrying his seed with her when she met their guests. "Fuck me, London, you're running out of time, baby."

Evan watched determination light in her glittering blue eyes as she wrapped her hand around the root of Evan's cock and sucked him so deep, he threw his head back and moaned her name deep in his throat.

"London, my love, next time I'm tying your damn hands down. Your touch sets my balls on fire. Swallow it all, baby. Swallow every drop I give you." As soon as Eli saw her throat working frantically to take the release shooting to the back of her throat, he pushed his fingers deep in her heat, curving them to press against her sweet spot.

London's body responded to his touch so quickly, Eli had barely had time to suck her clit between his lips when the first rush of honey washed over his fingers. Moving lower, he lapped at the sweetest nectar he'd ever tasted, letting the earthy scent imprint itself on his very essence. Climbing up quickly, he positioned the tip of his cock at her entrance and watched Evan collapse beside her.

"You just stole another piece of my soul, baby. I'll never be the same. Fucking hell, if you get any better, you'll kill me."

Eli doubted his brother saw London's impish smile—from the glazed look on Evan's face, his eyes probably weren't focusing yet. Chuckling to himself, Eli reached forward, clasping her pink nipples between his fingers to give them a quick pinch. Rather than the gasp he'd expected, London's body shuddered as she closed her eyes and moaned.

"You are a gift from the gods, Princess. Such a perfect response to the edge of pain we're going to love exploring with you." Pushing himself in a fraction of an inch, Eli struggled to keep from plunging in balls deep and fucking her so hard, neither of them would remember their name. "Your pussy is trying to pull me deeper. I'm going to accommodate it soon, but first, I want you to look at me, love. Keep your eyes on mine while I fuck you. I promise to make sweet love to you later, but you have burned through every morsel of my control until there is nothing left but ashes."

Pushing himself further into her wet silk, Eli felt his wolf clamoring for release, but instinct told him London wasn't ready for their claiming yet, so he steadied himself with several deep breaths. Leaning forward, Eli wrapped his long fingers around her wrists, pushing her hands up over her head. She'd closed her eyes when the hair on his chest brushed over the tips of her taut nipples. "Eyes on me, Princess." The instant her gaze locked on his, Eli began thrusting deep enough to press his tip against the opening of her womb before retreating far enough the rigid ring around his cock head pressed against her G-spot. Hard and fast, followed by slow and sensual, he varied the thrusts until he felt her go liquid around him.

"That's it, Princess. Let go, I've got you. *Always.*" At the first clench of her vaginal muscles, Eli picked up the pace. Long, hard strokes coming faster and faster, he worried his mind was going to explode from the pleasure. "Your orgasm belongs to me, London. Come now." His command was met by her immediate response. She'd kept her eyes on his, but once the pleasure exploded around her, he knew she was no longer seeing anything happening around her.

Her vaginal muscles quaked around him, yanking him over the edge of release with her. Hearing her cry out his name was the last thing he remembered before searing heat exploded from his balls, racing up his spine to turn his brain to liquid lava before shooting back down again and erupting in a bolt of lightning. His cum shot from his cock with such violence, he was sure his body would never recover. His arms trembled from spent isometric energy, and he locked his elbows to keep from collapsing onto London's limp form.

"I'll move as soon as I can do so safely, Princess. You fried so many of my brain cells, it may be a few minutes before they're able to reboot." He heard Evan's soft chuckle to the side and realized his brother was holding two towels—one was damp, giving Eli the pleasure of cleaning his seed from her tender tissues, the other a soft, dry cloth to blot away the moisture before they returned downstairs. Groaning to himself, he wasn't sure he was going to be able to move out of his private quarters before the group downstairs gave up and returned home.

Don't even think about ducking out—Mom's already sent

several messages, you know what comes next. Oh yeah, he knew, alright. She'd send Dad Jameson up to retrieve them. Dad Jack would show up, asking for a snifter of brandy and watch the game on television until his lovely wife stomped upstairs to bring them all to heel. *Get a move on, I don't want mom pissed at me because your brain is off-fucking-line.* Groaning, he managed to lift his hand enough to give Evan a clear view of his middle finger before taking the two towels from his outstretched hand.

"I can tell when you are doing that, you know." Eli and Evan both looked up to see London leaning back on her elbows, studying them. "The air around you crackles with energy. I can feel the static electricity and know you are communicating telepathically." Eli was astonished and knew his surprise must have reflected in his expression when she giggled. "I'm going to remember this moment because I doubt anyone sees the two of you speechless very often." Her soft giggle melted something inside his heart and suspected she'd done the same to Evan.

You know, we've laughed at other Doms for having this look on their faces. I see it on yours, and I'm sure mine is the same. Fucking hell, I'd sell my soul to hear her laugh again.

Evan couldn't have agreed more as he watched Eli move to the closet and pull out the dress and shoes he'd selected for her to wear. When he stepped back into the bedroom, he grinned when her attention zeroed in on the shoes he was holding.

"Holy mile-high stilettos. Those shoes are beautiful, but…" He didn't give her a chance to finish, waving away what he assumed was a protest about the expense—after all, who the hell knew shoes could be so damned expensive.

"They'll make your legs look amazing, Princess. Come on, we need to get you dressed and downstairs before our mom sends Dad Jameson to drag us out of here." When he saw her look longingly at the bathroom, he shook his head. "You don't have time for a shower, but we'll give you ten minutes to fix your hair and makeup. You'll find everything you need in the top drawers." When she reached for the dress, he shook his head. "Not yet. We plan to keep you naked as long as possible." Watching the swirl of emotions in her eyes, Evan wondered which was going to triumph— arousal, embarrassment, or rebellion. She stood still, staring at the dress and shoes for long seconds before her shoulders shrugged, and she walked silently into the bathroom.

"I told you she was amazing although, in hindsight, I think I might have underplayed it." Evan was standing to the side, grinning like a damned fool. Eli looked at him and chuckled.

"You did warn me, but you definitely understated how terrific she is. I was surprised she seemed to be bothered by the shoes. She needs to learn to accept gifts because I'm going to enjoy dressing her." *Speaking of understatements….*

"You should have let her speak because I suspect her protest wasn't about the money." Eli raised a brow in question and waited for Evan to continue. "It's the heels. She's a lab-rat, Eli. She hasn't spent her career navigating boardrooms, offices, and kink clubs in fuck-me heels." Eli's eyes widened at Evan's observation. *That goes a long way to explain the butt ugly shoes I found in her bags.* Evan suspected the footwear had been well worn, which had no doubt led

Eli to believe she hadn't had the time or the money to buy anything new. The shoes might have been about comfort, but Evan wondered if her clothing reflected her insecurity rather than a preference for shoes allowing her to work all day on concrete or tile flooring.

LONDON STOOD LOOKING at herself in the mirror, shocked to see a woman she barely recognized staring back at her. Her cheeks were flushed, her eyes clear and sparkling with something London wasn't sure how to describe. She'd seen the same luster in Brooklyn's eyes when she'd visited her sister and future brother-in-law at their New Mexico home several weeks ago. She hadn't understood then, but now she knew the look was sexual satisfaction... probably the wattage of the glow was directly correlated to the number of orgasms. The more times you got off, the higher your level of eye and skin radiance.

"Stop overanalyzing everything. You're wasting time. Who knows, Elijah might be one of those people who actually keeps track of time. Why is it such a big deal, anyway? Just because orgasms registering on the Richter Scale are new to you, doesn't mean the look is special. Probably no one downstairs will even notice. There won't be any way for them to know what we were doing up here." She'd already touched up her makeup and French-braided her hair, so the only thing left was using a warm cloth to wipe away the salty remnants of sweat. She looked longingly at the shower while smoothing thick, scented lotion over her arms and legs.

"Don't even think about it." London gave a startled yelp, tightening her fist around the tube of cream, sending an arcing stream of what was probably very expensive skin moisturizer several feet in the air. Eli's eyes widened before softening. "Sorry, Princess. I wasn't trying to startle you."

"Damn and double damn, I'm sorry. I'll clean it up." She reached for another towel, but his large hand stilled her movement.

"No, love, leave it alone. The staff will take care of it when they come up in a few minutes. I've asked them to do a few things before we return, they'll take care of it for you."

"But that's not fair, they shouldn't have to clean up a mess I made because I wasn't paying attention." Her eyes darted to the side, and he waited, hoping she'd admit what was really bothering her. She remained silent for several seconds but finally huffed out a breath. "You didn't… well, you didn't hear me talking to myself, did you? I spend so much time alone, sometimes I catch myself verbalizing my thoughts aloud… it helps me process." Suddenly, realizing she was naked while he was fully dressed, London felt her face flame and ducked her head.

"No, London. Don't look away from me. Tell me what you're thinking and don't edit." His voice had taken on the same quality she'd heard earlier, the compelling undertone she was powerless to resist.

"I was hoping you didn't think I was a rubber room escapee. My family always looks at me indulgently when I talk to myself, but I know they think I might not have all my ducks in a row most of the time." Shaking her head, she smiled up at him but wasn't sure she'd managed to be convincing. "Who am I kidding, my ducks aren't even all in the pond much less in a row." Rubbing her forehead in frustration, London looked to where Evan stood at the door.

"We're going to discuss this again, Princess, but right now we need to get downstairs. There are several people who are very anxious to meet you." Eli led her to where Evan stood holding the dress they obviously planned for her to wear.

At least the fabric doesn't look as sheer as the last one. Maybe the dress gods sent something with a built-in bra and panties.

Chapter Thirteen

E VAN WATCHED LONDON walk on shaky legs closer to the main part of the house. She was struggling to maintain her balance in the sky-high heels, and he knew she was looking forward to taking them off. He'd was grateful he'd had the foresight to assure her that she could take them off as soon as the introductions were made. Despite her peevish muttering, he knew they would boost her confidence—if she could manage to stay on her feet. Damn, her grumbling was cute, and for now, it served a purpose. As long as she was focused on staying upright, she wasn't worried about meeting their parents.

Everybody in the damned room is going to smell us on her. Eli's gloating tone made Evan want to roll his eyes at his brother's caveman attitude. Fear was also a scent Evan knew every other pack member in the room would identify—the tangy aroma becoming stronger with every step they took. It wasn't surprising she was nervous, hell, it was to be expected under the circumstances. Unfortunately for London, the brave face she was putting on wasn't going to fool anyone.

We need to get her calmed down before we walk through the door, or she's never going to feel comfortable. She's going to be surrounded by virtual strangers, Eli. She won't stay with us unless she feels like she's got her feet under her. He was speaking figuratively as well as literally, and he hoped like hell Eli was listening. Caring for a mate took in a wide range of concerns, and in Evan's view, London's physical safety was only a small part of that responsibility.

I'm listening. My connection to our mate is already starting. I can sense her emotions but can't hear her thoughts yet. Eli directed them into one of the several bedrooms near the end of the hallway. Turning London, so she faced them, Evan felt like he'd been kicked in the chest at the anxiety he saw etched in her expression. Knowing Eli needed to strengthen his bond with her as quickly as possible, he would let his brother take the lead—this time.

"Tell me what you're thinking, London." Eli's simple question was all it took for the first tear to breach her lower lid to race down her flushed cheek.

"I know you think I'm nervous about meeting your friends and family, but that's not an insurmountable problem… after all, I grew up in a big family."

"Princess, you've only told us what *the problem isn't*—we need to know what *is* bothering you if we're going to help you resolve it." Eli's comment was so typical Dad Jameson it was almost comical. As far as Evan knew, their mother had never made any attempt to prove which one of her husbands had fathered her children. Both men considered the boys their own, but it had always been evident to Evan. Eli was a carbon copy of Jameson Monroe—in looks and personality—whereas, Evan favored Dad Jack.

"I don't want to fall down." The words had tumbled out so quickly, they took both Evan and his brother by surprise. "Shit, I'm sorry, I really should have tried to phrase that… umm… differently, but I'm not really good at this stuff." Chewing on her lip, Evan watched her eyes dart around the room, focusing on anything and everything—except them.

"First, I want to point out you have done remarkably well navigating a long hall with very little help from us. Second, you are assuming we're going to leave your side—we won't. And third, this is a very select group, Princess. Everyone wanted to meet you, but we only invited a few people because we didn't want to overwhelm you."

What Eli wasn't telling her was their invitation had become the hottest ticket in town overnight. Every member of the pack was anxious to meet London. Their reasons were varied—some wanted to see if she was worthy, others wondered what sort of woman had finally appealed to two men who were so different. Unfortunately, there were also a few members who were foolish enough to believe they could challenge London for the position as their mate.

London took several deep breaths, straightened her shoulders, and looked at the door. "Let's do this. I want out of these damned shoes."

***

LONDON'S HEAD WAS spinning like a damned top. *How many names do they expect me to remember? And didn't someone say this was an intimate group… as in not a large number of people? There has to be close to forty people here!*

Sending out a silent prayer of thanks to the Universe

for her photographic memory, London was convinced it was the only thing keeping her from running screaming out the front door. So far, she hadn't forgotten anyone's name—a huge win in her view. She'd been introduced to more than thirty people, and she wondered if more were making their way inside when no one was looking. There were times London would go days without seeing anyone except the custodial staff at the lab, and to be honest, more often than not, the solitude suited her just fine. She didn't consider herself anti-social... London preferred to think of it as 'selectively social.'

"London, I'd like to introduce you to my parents." Evan's breath brushed over the back of her neck, making her shiver with sexual awareness. Her body was readying itself for him before her mind registered the word *parents*. *Parents! Yikes! Pay attention, London. Horny and parents do not belong in the same thought.* Evan coughed to cover his snort of laughter, but she thought the move needed work since his parents seem more amused than fooled.

The four of them exchanged pleasantries, but it was Jack Monroe who captured her attention. "London, I was sorry to hear about your parents' passing. Your father and I worked on a few... projects while we were in college, and I met your mother a few times before we all graduated. They were so in love, I wasn't surprised to hear they'd gotten married and started a family."

London was shocked, she'd never met anyone who'd known her parents aside from the few people who'd come to the funeral. For several seconds, all she could do was stand in stunned silence.

"Thank you. My brothers, sisters, and I miss them very

much. I'd love to hear more about your time with my dad, I've never talked to anyone who knew him in college. By the time I came along, I'm afraid they didn't have much time for socializing, so this is a rare opportunity for me to hear what they were like before they were turned into super-parents." In her peripheral vision, London saw Jameson Monroe frown at his brother, but Jack seemed to take it in stride.

"I'd be happy to tell you what little I know. Give me a couple of days to think back, then we'll have lunch—but I can tell you this much, your father was one of the smartest men I'd ever met. He seemed to be on the fast-track to a political career before he fell in love with your mother." She must have looked confused, because he quickly continued, "Your mother was a flower child long before it was a *thing* as you young people say. As I'm sure you know, your mom had a gift. Some might call it insight, but it was more than that. Season knew how easily souls were corrupted by politics, and she wanted nothing to do with it and swore she was saving Matthew from a life filled with nothing but heartache."

"That sounds exactly like something my mom would have said." Reaching out, she placed her hand on his forearm to thank him for taking the time to share a memory with her. Jack had gone above and beyond to make her feel welcome. She didn't get the chance to utter a sound because the moment her fingers came into contact with his warm skin, images began swirling through her head. The jumble was so disjointed, London couldn't make any sense of what she was seeing. In the back of her mind, London could hear people shouting to her, but they were so far away, she couldn't make out what they were saying. She felt herself swaying and wanted to curse the damned heels she was still wearing. Blinking her eyes in a futile effort to push the collage of pictures back from her vision, London felt herself falling and wondered who'd turned out the lights.

"WHAT THE HELL?" Eli saw London reach out to Dad Jack, then he'd been slammed with wave after wave of confusion. He was already moving across the room when he saw Evan catch her in his arms. Dad Jack was leaning against the counter, looking shell-shocked as his brother and wife looked on in confusion. Following Evan into his office, Eli closed the door behind them and was grateful for their dads' wisdom when they'd soundproofed the room.

"Is she okay? What on earth happened?" He followed Evan who settled London on his lap after sitting on the overstuffed sofa. Eli moved to the heavy oak table in front of them and reached forward to brush aside the stray tendrils of hair that had worked free of her braid. Relief flooded him when her eyes fluttered open.

"Baby, can you tell us what happened?" Evan's question echoed his own, and Eli was grateful his brother already had a strong connection with their mate, hoping Evan was picking up additional information from their close physical contact. London blinked several times as if trying to clear her vision, but Eli could feel the confusion she was trying to shake off.

"I'm not sure. I was so grateful your dad had shared a

memory about my parents, I reached out to thank him, but as soon as I touched him… I felt like I'd been hit by lightning. The surge of power wasn't frightening, it was… damn, I really don't have any words to describe it." As she'd been speaking, their parents stepped through a door behind her. Eli doubted she'd noticed the secondary entrance, it was well concealed as a security measure.

"Perhaps we can help." Eli watched London struggle against Evan's hold as she tried to get to her feet. Grinning, Eli watched Evan slip his hand under her dress and felt rather than saw her surprise.

"Stay still, or I'll leave my hand where it is—and just so you know, if my fingers are laying against your pussy, I'm going to play." Eli watched as London went stock still, her breath catching as her pupils dilated with arousal. Evan glanced at Eli and groaned. *Our woman just soaked my fingers. Damn, I can't wait to push her boundaries.* Eli had to bite back his laughter at the knowing looks on their dads' faces.

Might want to dial it back a notch before Mom's awareness catches up with the dads. Their mom was hurrying across the room, her hands wringing in front of her, Dad Jack close on her heels. He knelt in front of London, giving her a sympathetic smile.

"London are you okay?" Dad Jack's voice was ripe with concern, but Eli noticed he was making sure he wasn't touching her.

"I think so, but I don't understand what happened." *Except that I should have kept my damned hands to myself. Talk about a huge not in Kansas anymore Dorothy moment.* Eli snorted a laugh at the same time Evan chuckled. It pleased him to know his connection was strengthening so rapidly; it also gave him new insight into the heart of their mate.

JACK THOUGHT HE'D seen it all. As a shifter, his lifespan was far longer than the average man's, and he'd always been of the mind you needed to pack all you could into the time you had on Earth. His father had preached to both of his sons the importance of life experience, stressing how central both good and bad experiences would help them be effective pack leaders. He had often worried he and Jameson hadn't passed along the importance of living life to the fullest to their sons. Damn if they hadn't always been ridiculously responsible and mature beyond their years.

He'd had a fleeting thought about Season Adler when he'd first heard his sons were sheltering her daughter, London. Later, he'd been so surprised to learn both of his sons were interested in the women the medical community was raving about, he'd pushed Season's long-ago words aside. Thrusting his hand through his hair, Jack stood and began pacing. He'd have preferred speaking privately with his sons before broaching this subject with London, but he'd lost the opportunity as soon as her delicate hand touched his arm. Taking a deep breath, Jack looked at his wife and sighed when she nodded.

"You have to tell her. It's okay, husband mine. Keeping London safe is more important than my pride." Jameson moved to stand behind his wife, wrapping his arms around her and pulling her back into his embrace. Sighing, Jack marveled at the woman who'd stolen his heart so many years ago.

"Would someone please tell us what's going on?" Jack looked at Eli and wished he'd taken Season's warning more seriously, but he'd been too young to fully understand gifts he didn't possess.

"I mentioned your father and I worked on a project in college, but I didn't mention when that was. I'm not sure how much you know about shifters..."

"At this point, I think it would be best to relay only the most critical points. London will have plenty of time later to learn the finer points of living in the shifter community." Jameson was right—as usual. Jack stopped pacing to look directly at London—moving closer but staying out her reach until she understood what she felt when they touched.

"I'm what the ancients called an *Enabler*. Now, with the negative connotations that term evokes, some refer to me as an *Anchor*." He appreciated the way she held the questions he could see swirling in her pretty blue eyes, giving him a chance to get the words out without jumping in. She reminded him so much of her mother, he'd had to pay close attention so he didn't inadvertently call her Season.

"For our purposes, I think the term Enabler is more accurate. Just out of curiosity, did you feel a similar sensation the first time you touched Evan?" At her quick nod, his son appeared surprised, but agreed electricity had seemed to pulse between them. London said she'd attributed the shock to attraction because something similar had taken place with Eli. "Don't discount the part physical attraction plays, but I also want to point out you said something similar when referring to Eli. Evan is an Anchor and Elijah is not. Elijah is the fire element just like Jameson. Evan is earth, just as I am."

Nervous energy was rolling through him, and before he realized what he was doing, he was on his feet again. Making two passes in front of the native stone fireplace, Jack was surprised to find London standing in his path when he turned to make a third.

"I know we only just met, but I'd like for you to trust me enough to simply tell me whatever is on your mind. Think of yourself as a teacher imparting knowledge to a very anxious student." She'd impressed him in a way very few people ever had. Jack smiled at London before looking at his sons.

"The Universe has given you an amazing gift. Treasure her always. We've worked hard to teach you the importance of honor and gratitude—don't forget those lessons." Returning his attention to London, he began by explaining the importance of balance in relationships. "There needs to be equitable power, but it can't all come from the same element, or the union will never last." Waving his hand between Jameson, Julia, and himself, Jack smiled.

"Jameson is fire—he is driven by an internal flame that burns brighter because he knows I'll always keep him tethered no matter how much the fire rages. Our lovely wife is air, just like our sweet London. People of the air element touch the future. London, until I met you, your mother was the strongest air person I'd ever met. Season touched the future because she treated every person she met as if they were the most important person in the world." London gave him a slow nod of agreement.

"There was a homeless family who lived near the campus—remember in the 1800s, families who were homeless were outcasts. No one in the family would make eye contact, their shame was so great. But when your mom walked up to them, they not only looked at her, but she was also able to engage them in a meaningful conversation that resulted in the father being hired by her grandfather's company. The family never spent another night on the street. Not only did the parents thrive, but both children became Oxford Scholars."

London smiled, nodding her understanding. "She had an uncanny way of drawing people out. My dad called her his little magnet." Jack waited—knowing the rest of what he'd said was going to register soon, and he wasn't disappointed. "Wait. Holy Hannah, did you say the 1800s? Then it's true. All the rumors, the vague historical accounts of shifters living greatly extended lives." Her gaze shifted to Evan and Eli, curiosity lighting her eyes before resignation dimmed them. "How old are you? Oh, dear, how many mates have you had? It must be awful watching them age and leave you so quickly." Evan moved quickly to stand in front of her, shaking his head.

"We are young, not as young as we appear, but we'll cover all those details later, baby. Since shifters mate for life, you can rest assured you are our one and only. Mating is something we're looking forward to sharing with you if you decide it's what you want. Your body will experience physical changes when our DNA joins yours. We'll answer all your questions, I promise, but right now, I'm anxious to hear more about your mother."

"I'm also interested in hearing what the hell happened

in the kitchen earlier." Eli's narrowed eyes told Jack his oldest son was slipping into what he and Julia called his Jameson-mode. His patience was wearing thin, and his analytical mind was so focused on a goal, nothing could distract him.

"I wasn't lying when I said your dad and I worked on a project together, London—the project was seducing your mother." Jack took a deep breath and gave Julia a regretful smile. "They say every experience—good or bad—forms a piece of your character, so I can't say I regret the time I spent with your parents. I certainly don't regret the path my life took after they moved to Texas. In fact, I was always grateful for your mother's vision. She knew a polyamorous relationship between the three of us would never have worked, and she was right. In that day and age, it was unusual for a woman to speak her mind the way Season did—she really was born a hundred and fifty years before her time."

"I think she was born to blaze a trail. She taught my brothers the importance of listening to the women in their lives—I think some of them learned the lessons better than others, but she tried to enlighten them. She encouraged my sisters to push themselves... making certain they would never have to rely on a man for anything financial."

"What about you, baby? Didn't she give you the same guidance?" Jack could have answered Evan's question, but he let London take the lead.

"She didn't have to. I was always driven... often too driven for my parents' comfort."

Her words didn't surprise Jack at all. London's spirit mirrored her mother's in ways that brought back a flood of memories he'd long ago forgotten. The break between the three of them had been gut-wrenching—he'd been angry far too long, only healing when Julia found her way into his and Jameson's lives.

"During our college years, your dad and I weren't the most dedicated students." Jameson harrumphed across the room, making Jack chuckle. "Our parents eventually decided they'd funded our shenanigans long enough and ordered us to complete our degrees and either return home or find gainful employment."

"Are you telling me, my dad belonged to your pack?" Jack nodded and watched her eyes widen in surprise. "He never mentioned his family, and the few times I heard one of my siblings ask, he quickly changed the subject. My mother rarely mentioned her family other than to say they didn't approve of her marriage, and she quickly lost contact with them."

"That's true although oversimplified. Your mother's family was old money—old European money. The van Salees were not thrilled with your mother's special abilities, considering her a witch—they tried to have her committed more than once. The Vanderbilts trace their roots to the van Salees—that should give you some perspective about what we're talking about." Smiling at her, Jack couldn't help marveling at how well she was coping with everything she'd experienced in the past couple of days. Hell, from what he'd heard, her life had been one challenge after another since her parent's accident—an accident that was still under investigation as far as he knew.

"Matthew and Jack decided seducing the wealthy daughter of American's new golden class sounded easier than finding jobs. But Season turned the tables on them. They both fell for her, but it turned out Season's gift was much stronger than anyone knew. She could see the future, in ways no one expected." Jack was pleased Jameson offered an explanation, hoping like hell the two of them could establish a strong rapport with the young woman their sons planned to claim.

Julia smiled when she finally spoke up. "I met your mother once years ago. We got on wonderfully. It was easy to see why Jack had fallen in love with her. I don't think we ever forget our first love." Jack watched Julia's expression turn wistful. "It was oddly comforting to know Jack had been taken with a woman I liked. I know it sounds crazy, but if she'd lived closer, I believe we'd have been great friends." London listened intently, but it was easy to see she was scrambling to put all the pieces together.

"I didn't date in college, but my sorority sisters dated each other's exes, and it didn't seem to bother them. But it sounds very different listening to you... why?"

Jack understood London's gift better than she did, but he hadn't stopped to consider she was still looking at the situation from a purely human perspective. Eli moved in front of her, taking her small hand in his.

"Shifters are possessive, Princess. Very possessive. My brother and I will joyfully share you with each other— jealousy will never be an issue, but I'm warning you now, another man touches what is ours, and it will be an enormous problem."

Jameson chuckled and shook his head at Eli's declaration. Jack agreed, their sons had some hard lessons to learn, but he and Jameson would always have their backs.

Hopefully, they could keep the harsher moments to a minimum.

"I want to know what happened in the damned kitchen. Dad Jack, I think we've got the general idea about your history with the Adlers. What I don't have is a fucking clue how it relates to London's experience a few minutes ago." Evan's frustration was understandable but very unusual. His physician son was usually the picture of control, his bedside manner a point of pride for him.

"As an Enabler, I act as a conduit. Energy from the Universe is funneled through me, it can flow in either direction. It's always the strongest in the beginning—when I first meet an *air* individual, and it is proportionate to their particular gift—thus the power surge London felt when she touched me. Until her gift fully manifests, she'll continue to feel the sizzle of electricity passing between us."

"You keep talking about a gift, but I've never had a special gift… unless you count intelligence, and to be honest with you, there have been times that's been a curse." When Evan and Eli flanked her, one encircling her waist, the other her shoulders, she sagged into their hold.

Take your mate upstairs. She needs time to sort through everything. Jack spoke telepathically to shield London from the communication. She already had enough to deal with. The boys nodded and began walking her to the door, but London put the brakes on, turning back to him.

"What about the pictures?" Damn, he'd hoped she wouldn't remember.

"Probably a mixture of memories and foretelling—both past and future. Your mom always insisted learning to tell the difference was the hardest part, but I believe it will be much easier for you." Jack saw Julia step forward to grasp London's hands in her own.

"Jack's right, London. Your gift is very powerful. I believe your biggest challenges will be ethical. It's going to be difficult to know when to step in and when to let the Universe play out the hand it dealt. You'll want to save everyone from life's inevitable pain, but before you rescue someone, you should always need to ask yourself if you're interrupting their karma." London's expression flickered with unease before she pasted on a weary smile, thanked them, and let her men lead her out of the room.

Jameson looked between Jack and Julia, his expression turning heated in two seconds. "Let's go for a run. I feel like fucking in the woods." The scent of Julia's arousal drifted around them, and Jack fought the urge to strip and take her over the desk. Reading his expression, Jameson shook his head. "We no longer have the right to take her in this office—that privilege belongs to our sons." Grasping Julia's hand, he pulled her toward the door. "I've already told Trin to lock up. Come on before I change my mind about the desk." Julia's giggle brought chuckles from both men as they raced to the back door.

Chapter Fourteen

A USTIN ADLER STOOD in the shadows, watching his brother flog one of the Prairie Winds Club submissives. The petite blonde's fair skin was covered with the vibrant pink lash marks Israel loved so much. The wide strips of the supple deer hide flogger would warm her skin, a deceptive warm-up before Israel changed the angle and intensity, but the pretty little brunette was already too close to la-la land to care. He and Israel maintained memberships to several clubs around the world, but Prairie Winds outside Austin, Texas and Dark Desires in Houston were the two Austin favored.

Israel was as sexually dominant as Austin, but their tastes were different in subtle ways. Israel played hard, provided tender after-care that turned even the most jaded subs into his most loyal admirers, and always walked away without ever looking back. Israel was always upfront with the subs he played with, letting them know during their initial scene negotiations their relationship would never be anything more than what they'd agreed on. His skill with a flogger and his ability to remain friendly with the subs he'd walked away from made Israel one of the most sought out Doms in several clubs around the country.

Lifting his gaze from the small stage, Austin's attention was drawn to a slender figure standing against one of the moveable walls the club used to reconfigure the vast space into smaller, more intimate spaces. She was partially shadowed, but there was something familiar about her. She was watching the scene, and he could feel the deep-seated need pulsing around her. The unmistakable aroma of sex had surrounded him since he'd walked through the club's front door, but the musky tendrils tickling his nose now were carrying a different scent—one that called to his wolf on such an elemental level, it was impossible to ignore.

"Do you know her?" Austin turned his gaze to the man who'd stepped up beside him and shrugged. A year ago, Austin would have been surprised to see club owner, Cameron Barnes, but since Cam and his growing family had moved less than five minutes down the road, he and his wife had become club regulars. Turning back, he felt the woman across the room studying him, her eyes widened in recognition a split second before she vanished in a silvery mist.

"What the fuck? Did she just disappear into thin air?" Austin had known Cam for years and could honestly say this was the first time he'd seen the former CIA agent flustered. "What the hell? Do you know her?" Austin hadn't answered the first time because he'd wanted to get a better look, and now the little brat had just made certain he wouldn't be able to confirm her identity. It took him several seconds to find his voice—he didn't know what had surprised him more, the fact she was in a kink club, or the shocking realization she'd just shimmered out of sight. He'd read about the magical ability in the ancient tomes, but he'd never known anyone who could do it.

"Yes, or at least I believe so. I could have sworn the woman was my assistant, but I had no idea she was into kink." In his peripheral vision, Austin saw Cam staring at him in disbelief.

"She fucking disappears into a shiny mist, and you're astonished she's into kink? Are you kidding me? Holy fucking hell. I want to meet her—arrange it. The implications of this are so far-reaching, I don't even know where to begin."

They'd been friends for years, and Austin couldn't remember Cam ever asking him for a favor, so there wasn't a chance in hell he would deny him the introduction, but he wanted answers from Ms. Charlotte Hays first—and he wanted them now.

"Excuse me. I'm going to find my vanishing right hand." Cam was still muttering in disbelief as Austin stomped around the perimeter, trying to make his way to where he'd last seen Charlotte when he'd felt her eyes locked on him. How he missed the fact she was a *magical*? And more importantly, how had she managed to hide her submissive side—because there had been no doubt in his mind the woman standing across the room was a sub. Fucking hell, need and desire had been coming off her in waves until she'd seen him watching her.

He would do his best to track her down tonight, but if she managed to elude him, she wouldn't be able to avoid him for long. Austin knew precisely when he'd have another opportunity—he knew exactly what time his admin would enter the Adler Oil inner sanctum Monday morning.

You cannot hide forever, Charlotte.

SHIT. SHIT. SHIT. I thought he said he was leaving town for the weekend? Fuckity fuck. She'd been so engrossed in Israel Adler's scene, she hadn't notice Austin standing across the room until it was too late. When she'd first arrived, Charlotte had asked if Austin was inside, but the man everyone called Tank had shaken his head and given her stern reminder about the strict confidentiality agreement she'd signed when she first joined Prairie Winds several months earlier. During her extensive research prior to joining the club, she'd learned the contract they called an agreement was one of the strictest in the kink world, and several of their associate clubs used the same document.

She appreciated the fact her membership at Prairie Winds would allow her to visit any of the other clubs in the network, offering a reduced membership rate if she should decide to join one of the other establishments. Of course, the only other club close enough for her to attend would be Dark Desires in Houston, and after the damned disappearing act she'd just pulled in front of club owner, Cameron Barnes, that option was probably off the table now.

Moving swiftly along the outer perimeter of the main room, Charlotte was careful to avoid bumping into anyone. Taking a deep breath, she tried to refocus. She needed to slow down, several people had felt the brush of air as she passed and turned to look, their surprise to find nothing but empty space clearly showing in their expressions. If Austin was looking for her, their reactions would give her away.

Charlotte had researched Austin for two years, studying his habits, likes, and particularly the things he disliked. Discovering he was a sexual Dominant had been a bonus in her opinion since it was something she had been reading about since she'd gotten her first e-reader. Smiling to herself, she thought about all the steamy novels she'd downloaded, often wondering if the small electronic device might someday spontaneously combust.

Looking behind her, Charlotte saw Austin was indeed following her and gaining fast, from the looks of it. Turning back around, she was surprised to see Tobi West standing close... much too close. Bumping into the petite blonde hard enough to knock her off-balance, Charlotte was forced to reach for the other woman to keep her from tumbling to the floor. The effort required to keep the vivacious woman she'd found herself drawn to from falling divided her focus. Damn it all to hell, maintaining a shimmer disappearance required a tremendous amount of concentration, and the effort to help Tobi and her haste to escape was simply too much.

"Holy shit-sus, Charlotte, I didn't see you coming." Tobi's voice held uncertainty because she'd been looking forward and would have seen Charlotte... if she'd been visible.

"Nobody saw her coming, Tobi." The chill in Austin's voice skittered up Charlotte's spine as he wrapped his large hand around her upper arm, steadying Tobi with the other. "Are you okay or would you like me to find one of your husbands?"

"I'm right here, Austin. Thank you both for keeping my lovely wife from tumbling to the floor." Kyle West stepped forward, wrapping his arms around Tobi, pressing a kiss to the top of her head. "I can't let you out of my sight for a minute, Kitten, you are a trouble magnet."

"I can assure you, this time wasn't your sweet sub's fault." Austin hadn't released Charlotte's arm, his grip firm but not so much he risked bruising her.

"Like I said, she is a magnet for mischief, it just finds her. It's amazing really." Shifting his attention from Tobi to Charlotte, Kyle tilted his head studying her. "I was standing across the room, not far from Austin a few minutes ago." *Oh shit.* She was so screwed. "I'm looking forward to hearing an explanation for what I saw but believe Austin has called first dibs. I'll wait but not long, so don't be a stranger, Charlotte."

"I'll set up something early in the week. Cam wants to talk to her as well." To anyone who didn't know him well, Austin's tone would have sounded impassive, but she wasn't fooled. Austin Adler wasn't going to be happy until he believed he'd uncovered every one of her secrets. She was going to have to think fast to keep from blowing her mission, and she didn't have everything in place to reveal her purpose.

Damn it all to hell, a few more months and she'd have had everything lined out. She should have double checked he'd actually left town. If she'd known Israel had returned to Texas, she'd have anticipated the change in plans, but since she didn't have access to his calendar, she hadn't realized he was home.

Standing beside Austin, she felt another presence and

turned to see Israel leaning casually against the wall beside her.

"What did you do, Miss Charlotte? Big brother looks like he's about ready to blow a gasket." He'd barely spoken the words, but she'd heard not only the question but the amusement underlying his casual tone.

Dandy, just what I need, two shifters interrogating me... and to add gas to the flame, let's make sure one is my boss, and the other a damned tracker who can spot deception at a thousand paces. Israel Adler was unnaturally good at his job, making her wonder what other gifts he possessed... aside from being a shifter. Neither of them knew *she knew* their secret. Nor did they know she'd watched them shift and run into the wooded area running along the Colorado River and around Lake Travis.

She'd dropped her shimmer when they stripped out of their clothes, their ripped bodies highlighted by moonlight were pure perfection. Thank the gods she'd been well hidden—the last thing she'd needed was for them to spot her. Making sure she'd been downwind, so they didn't scent her, she'd felt a rush of moisture soaking her panties at the sight of their long cocks swelling as their bodies shifted. She'd heard the two brothers often shared their lovers but didn't know whether or not it was true since she'd made a concerted effort to avoid the club when she knew they might be in attendance.

Hearing a growl from Austin, Charlotte looked up at the man still holding her arm and blinked in confusion. Had he asked her a question? Oh hell, she'd been so busy thinking about how amazing he and Israel looked naked, she'd zoned out. Deciding to apologize to the woman she'd nearly knocked on her ass, Charlotte turned to Tobi and smiled.

"I'm really sorry I bulldozed you. I was looking behind me instead of where I was going. You'd think I'd learn, but it seems I'm doomed to a life of being a perpetual klutz." Trying to gently wiggle her arm free as she spoke hadn't worked, the damned man kept his enormous paw securely wrapped around her bicep. *Pun intended*. A snort of laughter from Israel made her gasp. Was he able to hear her thoughts? As unlikely as it seemed, she knew Brooklyn's fiancé was a gifted empath, so it wasn't impossible.

Israel stepped closer, grasping her other arm, mirroring Austin's hold. She suspected the two men were communicating telepathically, but there was no way to be sure. Israel flashed her a smile that told her he was either listening to her thoughts or too damned observant for his own good... and neither option boded well for her.

"Let's go. We need to have a long talk." *We? Need? Nope.* Leaning down, so his warm breath caressed the shell of her ear, Austin whispered, "I'd blank my mind for a bit if I were you—no reason to give my brother any more ammunition."

So, he does read minds... just fucking dandy.

Chapter Fifteen

"WHERE'S DAD JACK? Or are the two of you using the divide-and-conquer strategy?" Eli leaned back in his chair, watching the man who'd been his mentor in every way possible. While he appreciated Dad Jameson's usual explanation and assurance that splitting up made sense because it saved everyone time, Eli hoped his father understood the excuse wouldn't fly this time around.

"Definitely divide and conquer but not for the reason you think." Jameson Monroe leaned against the natural stone mantle over the fireplace, just as he had for decades. He and his younger brother, Jack, had led their pack through tumultuous times of change and had only recently retired, turning over the reins to their two sons. "Evan's work is every bit as important as yours—it's different but equally significant to the future of the pack. And the Universe has sent you an amazing mate—but you need to know all the backstory if you're going to keep her safe."

"I'm listening, but all I'm hearing is justification for the two of you splitting up. If this is supposed to save time, it isn't working." Eli and Jameson were usually more of a like mind, but today was an exception—knowing whatever his dad had to say related to London was stealing the last shred of his usual calm reserve.

"Patience is a virtue, my son. It took me far too long to figure out how important it was to watch and listen—hell, to let things play out in their own time. I've always hoped you would learn from my experience—from my mistakes as well as my success." So much for his dad getting on with it.

"Jack was honest with you about his relationship with Matthew and Season although he understated how badly he was hurt when they chose a traditional mating rather than including him." Eli had suspected as much—the pain in Dad Jack's eyes had been easy to see.

"I appreciate he didn't elaborate on that part of their history, it would have served little purpose except to make London feel guilty for something she had no part in." As a true submissive, London naturally craved harmony—knowing she would have always felt in some way responsible for Jack's heartache would have been an unnecessary stumbling block in their relationship. If he and Evan were going to convince her to stay, she needed to feel accepted, and he and Evan needed all the information they could get to make it happen.

"I feel like there was something very significant that wasn't said in your conversation with London last night, and I want to know what it is." His dad nodded his understanding and straightened to his full height before moving to one of the leather wingback chairs facing Eli's desk.

"Jack met with Season the night before she and Matthew were scheduled to move to Texas. I don't know all the details because he's never talked much about it, but I do know her parting words have always haunted him."

The background report Eli had requested on London hadn't contained much about her gifts since the bulk of the information came from the non-shifter world. Most of what he'd learned had come from Luke Grayson via Evan.

"Season begged Jack to take care of her daughter. She'd insisted he'd have an opportunity to help save her life when Season was no longer able to help." Elijah felt his eyes widen in surprise as questions began swirling in his mind. "Season insisted Jack's pack would play a critical role in her daughter's future, and for years, Jack tracked Season's growing family, wondering which one of the girls would need his help." Pushing to his feet, Jameson began pacing along the wall of windows—a habit he'd had for as long as Eli could remember. His dad always insisted he thought better when he was moving, and Eli found the ritual helpful as well.

"When we learned Brooklyn had been injured and treated at the clinic, Jack assumed the obligation had been fulfilled. It seemed as though Season's warning had only marginally missed the mark since Jack hadn't been personally involved. When we heard about London, he knew he'd been wrong. London is the one he's meant to help, but he's not sure what to do." Pausing, Jameson seemed to be gathering his thoughts, and Eli fought to remain quiet.

"Her work is going to make her a target for a long time, but it's also going to forever alter the way big pharma is viewed and operates. She is set to expose the dark side of a multi-billion dollar a year business, secrets they can't afford to be exposed will be front page news for months. London will be a hero to many, but others will consider her the worst sort of liability."

"I'm waiting for you to get to the point, Dad. So far, very little of this is new information and even less is significant enough to merit the mystery you've alluded to." His dad nodded, sighing in apparent frustration.

"Franklin Cordesi has been calling everyone who might help him connect with London—including Jack." *What the fuck?*

"Why would the man everyone suspects set up the attack on London call Dad Jack? Hell, how would he even know it was an option? If he was going for one of the former leaders, he'd call you." His dad nodded but ran his hand through his hair and began pacing again.

"We've known the Cordesi family for many years. They were allies before our ancestors moved to the New World, and we've stayed friends. We help one another when we can, but we've kept our business and personal lives separate. Franklin's father was a college friend of Matthew and Jack. It seems they were casual friends, but evidently, Franklin considers the connection enough to warrant a favor."

"What did he want?" When his dad didn't answer immediately, Eli growled deep in his throat and jumped to his feet. "What did he ask for, Dad?"

"He wants to talk to London. He swears his goal changed once he met her. I believe it's possible his personal view changed, but I think it was a process." Eli was more inclined to believe the man fell for London suddenly—he knew how he'd reacted the first time he met her. "Jack made it clear any decision would be made by London." Eli went still—hell, he wasn't even sure he was breathing.

Jameson held up his hand, forestalling any protest, and

Eli pulled in a deep breath, focused on remaining calm. He knew she'd cut Cordesi off without a backward glance, but he worried she would feel pressure to meet with him in a misdirected effort to prevent him from continuing to contact Dad Jack.

"Cordesi also tried to contact Austin Adler, but he was unavailable. It's my understanding he spoke with London's sister, Asia." Jameson chuckled, the sound centering Eli's attention. He watched his dad's expression soften before he continued.

"I met Asia Adler when she was fresh out of law school, then saw her at a Council meeting a couple of years ago. She's a force of nature with a quick, brilliant mind, and I'm not sure I'd ever met a woman as articulate. Surprisingly, she is also one of the most naturally submissive women I've ever encountered. It's an interesting contrast. When I heard about Matthew's accident, I wondered if she had a shoulder to lean on." Shaking his head, Jameson appeared to pull himself out of the contemplative state he'd fallen into, and Eli wondered how Asia Adler had managed to make such an impression on a man who was usually all business.

"Anyway, I wanted to forewarn you—I didn't want you to be surprised when Asia shows up at our front gate. I strongly suspect she won't want to take anyone's word when it relates to her little sister." His dad's expression was so overly confident, Eli suspected he already knew Asia was on her way. Although he'd rather spend his time with London, he'd deal with her sister if need be. Damn, he'd only been away from London for a few hours and already aching for her.

"What do you think we should do about Cordesi?" Eli already knew the answer, but he wanted to hear his dad's take on the situation.

"I agree with Jack. It needs to be London's decision. You can't take that away from her, son. Even if you'd already claimed her, I'd give you the same advice. If she decides to meet with him—and I believe she will because she'll feel the need to protect everyone else from the man's tenacious pursuit—the meeting needs to be supervised and on our turf."

Eli blew out a breath and nodded. He'd fight tooth and nail to keep London from meeting with Cordesi alone, and he was relieved to hear his dad was on the same page.

ASIA ADLER SLIPPED into the leather seat of her rental car and sent up thanks to the sweet angels of the Universe who'd inspired the invention of heated seats. She'd forgotten how cold it was in New England in the fall and winter... and most of the damned spring. Her South Texas blood was too thin for this nonsense. She programmed the luxury car's GPS to the hotel where she knew Franklin Cordesi was staying.

Their first conversation had been stilted. Asia had been damned skeptical when Cordesi called to speak with Austin, then insisted on being transferred to her. She'd already been running late for a meeting, so their conversation had been cut short with her promising to return his call, and she had... after reading the file and notes her future brother-in-law, Luke Grayson, sent at her request.

Damn it was handy having a hacker in the family. Luke's official title might not include that particular tidbit, but it was a simple semantic oversight.

What she'd read both infuriated and intrigued her, and while she regularly found herself annoyed with people, she couldn't remember feeling this challenged or interested in anyone in a long time. During their second call, he anticipated her questions and known she'd waited to call until she had more information. He'd chuckled when she'd tried to paint his profession in a negative light, telling her they were more alike than she was admitting. Pointing out they both advocated for their clients in any way they could, charged them handsomely for the service, then ordinarily walked away unscathed no matter the result. She'd been surprised when he'd blown out a weary breath and admitted the situation with London was anything but ordinary.

"I didn't anticipate the affection I developed for her, Ms. Adler. I'm not in love with London, but I'm certainly fond of her. I would like very much to help her stay safe."

She'd heard him sigh during a pregnant pause. As he'd continued speaking, she hadn't been able to take her eyes off the pictures Luke had included in his report. Cordesi might be English by birth, but his dark hair and olive skin were a testament to the dominance of the Italian gene pool. There was a picture of him sitting at a small metal table with the Eifel Tower in the background she kept returning to.

Everything about the picture was enchanting—the setting, the woman walking past on the sidewalk whose head was turned checking him out as she passed on the street, and the adoring look the male waiter gave Cordesi as he set a tumbler of amber liquid on the table in front of him. Clearly, his appeal wasn't limited to women although there was no indication in the file the man was bi-sexual. But it was the couple sitting with him that continually drew Asia's eye.

The man in the picture looked like an older version of Franklin, a much older brother or perhaps a well-aged father. There were enough physical similarities to assure her this was a man he knew well. Everything about the man's posture screamed dominance—the upward tilt of his strong chin, the way his arm wrapped possessively around his slender companion, and the way his thumb appeared to be tracing the pulse point inside her wrist.

There wasn't a woman alive who wouldn't recognize the man sitting with Cordesi as a sexual Dominant. The diamond choker around the woman's neck looked suspiciously like a collar, and Asia wished she could read the inscription on the small heart laying in the hollow of her throat.

Asia took great pride in the fact she always tried to be honest—particularly with herself—but admitting the spark of interest she felt every time she thought about Franklin Cordesi wasn't easy. After all the trouble he'd caused in her family, Asia felt a pang of guilt, knowing she was oddly attracted to a man who had at one time considered her little sister an assignment.

"With my back against the wall, I needed to bring her on board quickly and made a bad—okay, atrocious, call." His words had startled her back to the moment, and she heard a note of sincerity in his voice that surprised her. She'd also heard an underlying tone of warning when he added, "They won't stop. You're talking about billions of dollars lost if her research reveals their secrets. Ms. Adler, I assure you, even with the limited amount of background information I was given, I can see they'll be dangling in the breeze with their pants down when she publishes her findings."

The colorful picture he'd painted in her mind had nothing to do with the subject at hand—Asia forced her mind away from the hot scene she'd watched last weekend at Dark Desires. Seeing one of the club's dungeon masters bind a male and female sub in the deep red rope before flogging them at the same time gave a whole new meaning to *dangling in the breeze*.

"Ms. Adler?" He'd pulled her back from the memory she'd become lost in, and Asia could only hope she hadn't been panting in the phone.

"Yes. Sorry, I'm at work, so distractions are more common than I'd like." She'd ended the call, promising to call London, relay the information, then update him on her decision. After disconnecting the call, she'd reshuffled her schedule for the next few days, and gone upstairs to the apartment she'd recently remodeled one floor below Austin's enormous penthouse suite. She'd persuaded her big brother to relinquish a small portion of his five thousand square foot home to create a two-story outdoor living area they now shared.

Asia found the immaculately designed and landscaped outdoor space settled her mind, and she spent as much time outside as she did inside when she was home. The view was stunning during the day and breathtaking at night... she'd slept on one of the cushioned loungers under the stars more nights than she'd admit.

Refocusing her attention on the drive, Asia was relieved to find the hotel was closer to Evan Monroe's clinic than she'd originally thought. As soon as she'd settled into the suite she knew her assistant had reserved, Asia would call Elijah Monroe to arrange a meeting with her sister. Asia had promised herself she wouldn't let Franklin know she was on her way, swearing off calling him until after she'd talked to London, but it was a temptation she was finding more and more difficult to fight.

FOR THE FIRST time since he'd arrived, Franklin was grateful his suite was on a lower floor of the opulent hotel he'd chosen on the outer edge of Boston. Traveling as often as he did, Franklin had become accustomed to residing on the upper floors of the high-end hotels he preferred, but what he'd initially seen as an annoyance had just turned into a wonderful perk. Looking down on the sleek, black, luxury coupe pulling to a stop in front of the valet stand, Franklin smiled when one long, slender leg emerged from the door as the woman he'd spoken with yesterday reached across the seat, gathering a briefcase and purse.

Asia Adler graciously accepted the hand the young valet had extended, and Franklin felt his entire body stiffen in response. Jesus, Joseph, and sweet Mother Mary, what was that about? She didn't belong to him, and he had no reason to care who touched her—but his reaction had been visceral. He'd known she was coming—Ms. Adler wasn't the only one with connections and friends with more access than integrity.

He'd seen photographs—official shots from the Adler Oil website and candid shots taken by Franklin's team when he'd been hired to bring London into the Consortium's fold. Before arranging their accidental meeting, Franklin had studied each of London's siblings. Knowing her family background had helped him establish an easy rapport that had come crashing down around him just a few weeks later. Hell, he'd spent more time preparing for their first meeting than he spent dating the brilliant Dr. Adler.

Studying Asia as her long, tan legs ate up the short distance between her car and the hotel's front entrance, he was close enough to see her shudder against the biting wind. The well-respected attorney apparently hadn't taken time to buy appropriate winter clothing if the thin coat she wore was any indication. *Those stilettos make your legs look amazing, pet, but a killer pair of leather boots would be much more practical.* As she sauntered confidently through the sliding glass doors, Franklin sent a quick message to his assistant, requesting a warm coat and boots be delivered to Ms. Adler's newly reassigned suite as soon as possible.

Smiling to himself, he wondered how the woman known as the Adler Ice Princess in professional circles, due to her steely resolve during negotiations, would react when she discovered her reservation had been changed. He'd paid the manager handsomely to have her moved to the suite next to his. Several additional large denomination bills bought him an electronic key which he'd used shamelessly earlier in the day to decorate the space with floral arrangements and her favorite foods.

After his conversation with her yesterday, he'd spoken with one of Adler Oil's competitors who'd described Asia as stone-cold, but Franklin disagreed. He'd heard something entirely different in her husky voice. There was an air of vulnerability beneath the confident veneer, a bubbling cauldron of need buried so deeply in her psyche, he doubted she understood its true depth. Worth their weight in gold, his team had outdone themselves when they'd uncovered Asia's Dark Desires membership. He'd visited the club on one of the nights he'd known she planned to be there. Standing next to his long-time acquaintance, Cameron Barnes, Franklin had shaken his head.

"He's not getting her out of her head." The Dom wielding the flogger was trying so hard to impress the woman tied in front of him—so caught up in his *performance*—he'd completely forgotten why he was there.

"I swear if she starts cross-examining him, I'm going to cancel both their memberships." Cam's droll comment was probably only partially muttered in jest. "She needs someone who will see past the Ice Princess façade she presents to the world. Her soul yearns for the release she only finds under the lash of a strong Dominant." Franklin knew Cam well enough to hear his frustration. Turning to him, Cam studied him for a few seconds. "Tell me about your latest assignment, and before you give me what I'm sure is a well-rehearsed sales pitch, I'll tell you I've been briefed by the Agency."

"Retired, my ass," Franklin chuckled because anyone who believed Cam Barnes wasn't still working for the CIA was either dangerously ignorant or deliberately sticking their head in the sand. "Is Asia under your protection?"

Franklin knew Cam had been known to adopt club members, but he hadn't heard anything connecting him in a substantial way to the Adlers.

"No, but Ian McGregor has taken Brooklyn under his wing, and I know he is also fond of Catalina—it goes without saying, Cooper is involved." Franklin had heard the rumors about Hicks and the lovely jewelry designer. Catalina Adler's sideline as an independent agent was one of the worst-kept secrets in the world. "Tell me about your assignment."

Franklin outlined how the contract had begun and how things changed after he'd gotten to know London. He might have been speaking to Cameron, but he hadn't taken his eyes off Asia. Cam had chuckled more than once at his lapse in attention, but Franklin hadn't been able to take his eyes off the beautiful woman who wasn't having her needs met. As the Dom released her bonds, Asia's gaze swept the room, her eyes locking on his, despite the fact he was standing deep in the shadows.

Electricity arched between them, and even though she didn't know it, at that moment, she'd become his.

Chapter Sixteen

"**W**HAT DO YOU mean I've been moved to another suite?" Asia stared in disbelief at the clerk, completely baffled. She'd just confirmed the reservation to her assistant in Austin, and since he hadn't mentioned anything about making a change, Asia was at a loss. "Was there a problem with the other suite?" There was no real reason for her to be upset, after all, it was just a place to sleep, but the obsessive control part of her brain didn't do well with changes she didn't initiate.

"No, Ms. Adler, there was nothing wrong with the other suite, but I believe you will find the new one is much nicer. Perhaps you'd like to see it first?" She could see the man was beginning to sweat, and the lioness in her smelled blood.

"Who initiated this change?" As the second oldest of ten, she was used to muddling in her sibling's lives, not having someone fuck with hers.

"The hotel manager signed the change, he will return in a few days if you'd like to speak with him." This conversation wasn't accomplishing anything, and all Asia wanted to do was collapse for a few minutes in a comfortable chair… a chair that wasn't moving. A glass of wine would go a long way to soothing her ruffled feathers.

"I'm tired. I just want to rest. Can you please have my bags delivered to my room quickly so I can settle in? I'd like to order room service now if that's alright." She reached for the key, but a suited arm reached around her before she could take it from the clerk's outstretched hand.

"Excuse me, I'll take that." Turning to confront the owner of the linen-suited arm, Asia felt her eyes widen in surprise. She recognized the man from the numerous pictures in the file she'd received.

"Mr. Cordesi, to what do I owe this pleasure?"

"IF YOU ARE looking for someone to blame for the suite change, begin with me." Nodding to the clerk, he returned his focus to the confused woman standing so close, he could smell the sweet scent of her shampoo. "Come." Without waiting for her to respond, Franklin wrapped his hand around her wrist. He was pleased with her response—the widening of her eyes a split second before they dilated, the hitch in her breathing, and the acceleration in her pulse pounding at the base of her throat—told him she would enjoy being bound in his cuffs. Giving her a gentle tug, he nodded when her feet were finally set in motion. "This way, *Cara.*"

"Dear? If you think I'm anyone's *dear*, you are woefully misinformed." She let him lead her to the elevator, and he was keenly aware of the difference in their size. Her five-foot-seven height and four-inch stilettos might make her a formidable presence in the courtroom, but she still stood well below his six and a half feet height. Franklin's olive skin, dark hair, and eyes were a nod to his Italian heritage, but his height and commanding presence came from his father's Norwegian roots.

Since they weren't alone in the elevator, Asia held her tongue—but he suspected her silence cost her a piece of her sanity. Franklin fought to keep his expression neutral. Frustration was practically vibrating around her. He would enjoy the quiet while it lasted because there wasn't a chance in hell it was going to last. He surprised her by stopping before they reached the door to her suite.

"This is my suite, *Cara*. I wanted you to be close by. There is a door between our main rooms—one I hope is open very soon." Her soft gasp told him far more than the deliberate upward tilt of her chin. *Oh yes, my lovely Cara. You and I were made for one another.*

LONDON WANDERED THROUGH the vast open area, trying to mentally picture how the room should be arranged. The list of lab equipment Evan and Eli had ordered was extensive—far more than she'd imagined. The company delivering the expensive equipment had designed the space and would set everything up, but she was having fun imagining how it would look this time tomorrow.

So far, the only part of the room furnished was a small seating and break area to one side. The upholstered partitions faced the lab, but on the other side, the utilitarian dividers were hidden by lush plants and expensive furniture. Looking up, London was surprised to find Eli standing alongside Evan, both men watching her so closely, it was almost unnerving.

Something about their focus told her they had news and were gauging her mood. Evan's explanation about the growing bond between them explained the whispers of awareness she felt with increasing frequency. Knowing she was beginning to learn to communicate telepathically was both exciting and terrifying. There were times she was petrified by her rapidly changing life and how easily things seemed to have spiraled out of control.

London should probably be concerned at how close the three of them had become in such a short period of time, but it was the one piece of the puzzle that seemed to fit so perfectly, she found it hard to worry about. Looking down at the new tablet they'd given her, she smiled once again at the extensive list of scientific equipment being delivered today. She wondered if they knew she'd probably lock herself inside and not emerge for days at a time.

"How much longer do you plan to wander around smiling at an empty space, Princess?" Eli's question may have sounded casual, but there was an undertone she wondered if he'd infused intentionally. He was obviously tired of waiting... but she wasn't sure what he was waiting for.

"I'd be a lot more patient if she was naked." Evan's tone was teasing, but his gaze blazed over her, and London could have sworn she felt the heat his lingering look left behind. Sucking in a deep breath in an effort to keep from stripping off her clothes and claiming the men she already considered hers, she tried to calm her raging libido. *Holy shit, what's wrong with me? All I have to do is see them, and I'm steamrolled by need.* Evan smiled indulgently and answered her unspoken question.

"It's a part of the mating process, baby. It will get much worse after we claim you. We'll spend weeks fucking as often as possible—any time, any place. It's expected." Another scorching visual caress smoothed over her, making London groan softly.

Gasping at his crude remarks, she shook her head, wondering if she would ever be able to speak so casually about sex. Turning to the wall of windows facing the courtyard, she grinned.

"This might be my favorite part of the entire lab… and that's saying a lot." London loved the natural light and appreciated the security of knowing she wasn't fully exposed to the outside world. "I haven't worked in a lab with windows since I was in college." Both men looked surprised and aghast—it was probably abhorrent for a shifter to be cut off from Mother Nature. "I was starting to feel like a mole at Gates. The entire place was like a dungeon, the only windows in my small lab faced a hall that was painted olive green and gray. Who on earth puts those colors together besides the army? And the entire building had fluorescent lighting that hummed all the time. The drone could lull you to sleep in minutes if you didn't drown it out with music." London knew she was rambling, but a feeling of foreboding was wrapping around her, tightening like bands of steel around her chest until she felt her breath starting to catch.

"Come here, Princess." Eli held out his hand, and London wondered why her feet were already moving before his words had fully registered. Either a part of her was sensing what they were going to command, or her damned feet were no longer connected to her brain. As she crossed the cavernous room, their distress became more oppressive, and London unconsciously slowed her steps.

I don't want to hear it. Whatever it is, I just want to hide and ignore it. Bad news is best delayed. She was a great believer in the ostrich theory. The last time she faced bad news head-on, she'd lost her parents. London always wished she'd delayed the inevitable for a few minutes longer, wished her life had been normal for just another hour or two. Dark spots were dancing in front of her eyes before she was close enough to reach for them, and she had the strangest feeling of detachment before everything went black.

EVAN CAUGHT LONDON in his arms and stood looking down at the petite woman who'd stolen his heart. "I tried to keep up, but fucking hell, her thoughts were pinging off the damned walls so fast, I barely realized she wasn't breathing in time to catch her." Eli moved in front of his brother and brushed her dark hair away from her pale face.

"She obviously sensed our disquiet over Cordesi." Evan was relieved London finally seemed as connected to Eli as she was to him but also realized they needed to be more diligent in shielding her from strong emotions. Shifters were known to be passionate creatures, prone to intense feelings and reactions, but London was much more cerebral. She'd spent years working in virtual solitude, it would take a time for her to acclimate. *Assuming she doesn't decide it's not worth the effort.*

"She read the tension and assumed we had bad news to share. I can't imagine how difficult it must have been for her to learn about her parents' deaths. She's far more intuitive than she knows. We'll need to approach things differently—at least until we've earned her trust. I want her to know we're her safe haven—her shelter in any storm." Eli's words reflected how Evan felt as well. He watched as his brother feather soft caresses down the side of her face until her eyes fluttered open.

"Welcome back, Princess. I wish I could turn back time a few minutes and erase the worry I see in your eyes, beautiful."

"We just wanted to talk to you about Franklin Cordesi, baby." Damn, he felt like a first-class ass.

It will take us time to learn her triggers, brother. Everyone has them, and as her mates and her Doms, it's our job to uncover them. We'll help her overcome or cope.

He knew Eli was right, but it didn't assuage the guilt he felt at upsetting her unnecessarily. Evan made a note to thank the staff for setting up the small seating area before the lab equipment arrived. It would have been easy for them to wait, but once again, their community had gone above and beyond. Settling her on his lap, so she faced Eli, Evan let his brother explain.

"It seems Mr. Cordesi wants to speak with you. He has called in favors from mutual friends, many of whom have given him glowing recommendations." He and Eli had both been shocked when they'd gotten calls from several of their friends, including Cameron Barnes.

"I can't imagine what he thinks we have to say to one another, but I feel bad knowing he is annoying you and your friends with phone calls." Eli shook his head and chuckled because this was exactly what both their dads had predicted. She was lost in her own frustration and didn't seem to register his reaction. "Sometimes I swear phones are the most annoying things ever." Three different ringtones sounded all at one time, London's mouth dropped open, and she slapped the palm of her hand against her forehead. "The phone gods are a real pain in my ass. I don't even have my phone, and I could swear that's my sister Asia's ring."

CAROLEE JOHNSON SLIPPED stealthily out from beneath the trees, seething at what she'd seen on the small screen in her hand. The drone she used to watch Evan Monroe's clinic compound was making its way back to her. The flying gadget's home feature would cause the expensive unit to fly right into the damned trees if she didn't move far enough out into the open. The Consortium was paying her handsomely for information, and she didn't want to risk destroying the small spy device.

She'd gotten proof Dr. London Adler was onsite, and for a price, she would even tell them what part of the building the hussy researcher would be working in. Carolee planned to do a little video editing before turning over the file—there was no reason to short herself the extra cash by letting them figure it out themselves. Gathering her equipment, she started the long trek back to her car. Having worked at the Monroe Clinic, she realized how vast the pack's land holdings were and was determined not to be caught spying on the man she considered hers. *As soon as the Consortium gets rid of Dr. Adler, I'll return to heal Evan's broken heart.*

The path narrowed under the dense canopy of trees, and Carolee found her steps slowing as uncertainty assailed her. "I don't remember this." She'd barely whispered the words, but she needed to remember to remain as quiet as possible. The only thing stronger than a shifters sense of smell was their hearing, so silence was even more critical than the unscented soap she'd been using for a damned week while she waited for an opportunity to find the elusive chemist.

I knew the bitch was a problem when her damned sister was Evan's patient, but he hadn't been able to see through her charade. Pretending she was here for her sister... as fucking if. She was here to snag a husband, and now, the slut is angling for two.

SETH STUDIED THE monitors as he tracked the Carolee Johnson's movements and wondered why the former nurse was sneaking through the wooded area along the outer border of pack land. Technically, she was still listed as a member of the community, so there was no reason to dispatch any of the security team to investigate, but it was still odd—very, very odd. He'd checked her file and hadn't seen anything logged on her profile to indicate a problem, but her behavior set off his internal alarms. Grabbing the phone, he dialed Evan's number.

Chapter Seventeen

ASIA WAITED THROUGH several rings, tempted to throw the damned phone against the wall when London's voicemail came on the line. What the hell was the matter with her? She'd been pacing like a caged lioness since Franklin Cordesi kissed her and walked out the door a half hour earlier. Since when did she get this unnerved by a kiss? Confounded man. Everything he'd done since she arrived had been calculated to keep her off-balance, and it was working—much to her chagrin.

Damn it, she knew better than to let a man get the upper hand. Hell, she hadn't even allowed the wanna-be Dom she played with last weekend get ahead of her—something Master Cam called her out on before she left the club. The whole situation would have probably been worse if it hadn't been for Austin discovering he didn't know his assistant as well as he thought he did. Asia smiled to herself. Damn, she was anxious to get back to the office and find out how that was playing out.

Letting a man take the reins in your life was a recipe for disaster. Repeating the mantra in her head, Asia wondered if she'd ever find a Dom who could fulfill her needs—the needs she'd never shared with anyone. Women had never done it for her, so she ordinarily considered men a necessary complication. *They might be necessary, but they're not in fucking charge of me.* Great, she'd turned into a cranky toddler in heels.

Pulling the clothes from her suitcase, Asia contemplated her limited choices. Why had she agreed to have dinner with him? Hell, Asia had been so startled to see him at the front desk, she hadn't been on her game during their entire conversation. Sighing to herself, she had to admit it was a relief to know she'd have a chance to find out what the hell was going on with London… and she had to eat, so… *Give it up, girl. At least be honest with yourself. You are attracted to him, and he pushes your buttons.* The only information he'd given up before stepping through the adjoining door was to assure her his interest in London wasn't, nor had it ever been romantic.

Asia and her sisters had long-ago agreed they would never poach or date one another's exes. She'd rounded on him the minute they entered her suite, determined to find out what the situation had been. He'd proceeded to back her against the door, pinning her with nothing more than his dark gaze. Even if she hadn't seen him talking with Master Cam at the club, she'd have known he was a Dom—every movement was calculated and purposeful. Everything about him drew her like a moth to a flame while her survival instincts were screaming about the danger. Asia remembered her mother reading them the story of Icarus. The Greek mythology about the boy who flew too close to the sun moved through her mind as she'd fought her almost overwhelming attraction to Franklin Cordesi.

"Cara, I am very fond of London. She is a wonderful woman, that's why I'm going to extraordinary lengths to speak with her. I'd like very much to be her friend, I'm worried about her. The group who hired me only cares about money—her life means nothing to them. They know how significant her work is—and they fear her. From the first ripples, the effects of her report will be catastrophic to their bottom line, and the follow-up confirmations will go on for decades. She is poised to change everything anyone knows about vaccines in this country."

His words had taken a lot of the starch out of her spine as her dad used to say. Asia's built-in bull shit detector had rarely been wrong, and she'd sensed nothing but sincerity. Hell, he knew more about London's work than Asia did, and that was damned humbling.

Shit, I do not need this complication in my life.

FRANKLIN WATCHED THE small monitor as the woman on the other side of the door paced the length of the room, muttering about all the reasons she should not have dinner with him. He could tell her it was a losing battle—she was as attracted to him as he was to her. The arc of electricity between them could light up half of Boston. While he loved the historic ambiance of their surroundings, he would much prefer having her dressed in little to nothing on a warm Caribbean beach. Her long, lithe frame would make anything she wore look good—but not as good as she'd look completely exposed to his appreciative gaze.

Asia Adler wouldn't be easy to tame, but she'd be

worth it. Yes, indeed, she would be worth every bit of frustration.

LONDON SIDESTEPPED FROM between Evan and Eli, making her way into the kitchen, leaving them fielding questions from the steady stream of people moving in and out of Evan's home. If the two of them wanted to be slick and snatch up her phone, they could just answer the damned thing too. It's not like she ever got calls from anyone interesting, anyway.

They'd brought her back to the house using the tunnel which would be all fine and good when the weather was an issue, but her realization she hadn't been outside in a few days made her feel as though her skin was crawling. London knew both men had been out running at night. They were tag teaming. Clearly, they didn't think she noticed them slipping in and out of bed in the middle of the night... or the shower running... or way the air shimmered between them when they communicated telepathically in the dark.

London had agreed to meet with Franklin, but she still didn't see the point. What no one knew was she already had enough data to support the paper she'd already written. Of course, it would have been nice to run a fourth set of cross-tests, but even London realized it was overkill. Other research teams would become involved, and even though London wanted to test all the markers she suspected were being hidden in the vaccines, those studies would take years.

The important thing was to get the information out… let the public know pharmaceutical companies were preemptively poisoning their children… setting them up to be medical puppets for the rest of their lives. Knowing all a CEO had to do was issue an order and thousands of adults could suddenly find themselves battling a life-threatening illness was terrifying. She'd identified a variety of triggers—some environmental, others chemical.

Theoretically, a patient could be prescribed a medication for arthritis later in life, the drug company could add the catalyst, setting off a chain reaction which ended up creating a cacophony of issues guaranteeing corporate profits for generations to come. Everything she needed to sound the alarm was on the flash drives she'd had in her hand the night Evan rescued her. All she needed to set things in motion was a laptop and internet access.

London hadn't told anyone she was ready to publish although, at this point, she probably should. She wasn't stupid or naïve, she'd known her life would be in danger if anyone knew she was close to finishing her project. The fact they thought she was so easily fooled was more than a little insulting. *Damn it, if you want to go out and run at night, just fucking say so.* Yanking open the door of the refrigerator with enough force to rock her up onto her toes, she reached inside and pulled out a soda.

"Everybody thinks I'm dimwitted. It's just plain damned insulting. Hell, it's a wonder I can tie my own shoes without help." A masculine chuckle behind her made London freeze.

"In their defense, this is a new dynamic—something they didn't believe was ever going to happen, despite their mother's repeated assurances." Jameson Monroe's words surprised London as much as his smile disarmed her earlier frustration. "You haven't gotten to spend any time with my lovely bride, but you will, I promise. I think you'll find her company comforting. She and your mother share a lot of similar characteristics."

"I miss my mom every single day. And I'm not just talking about her sage advice and unconditional love. I miss the energy that always seemed to surround her."

"The effervescence?"

She must have looked surprised he'd understood. He grinned, and she found herself sucking in a sharp breath at the difference it made in his appearance. She was certain she'd just been given a glimpse at the young man he'd once been. All vestiges of the taciturn businessman she'd seen earlier evaporated for a few seconds, and she saw the man Julia had fallen in love with.

"Julia calls it sparkle, but it's more—sparkle implies surface shine, but Season's and my lovely mate's comes from a place much deeper."

London hadn't ever considered there was a difference in the terms, but he was right. Effervescence made her think of bubbles lining the inside of a glass, the entire surface covered as the tiny pockets of energy waiting to pop at the surface, sending bits of liquid bouncing in the air. It had been the same with her mother, the energy bubbling up from the depths of her soul to rain down on anyone close by.

"I agree there is a difference although I hadn't considered exactly what it was about my mom that drew people to her until you mentioned it." London smiled in gratitude.

His kind words meant more than he knew.

"Your work is important, London. More important than you know. Sadly, you are all too aware of how short life can be—tomorrow is promised to no one."

He was right, she'd learned the lesson in one of the hardest ways possible. Her parents had seen themselves surrounded by grandchildren in the future and traveling again after years of being *stuck* in the same location, but those dreams had been tragically erased in the blink of an eye.

"I know your paper is ready to publish. Get it out there. Those who want to cause you harm will be forced to change their focus from prevention to recovery."

"How did you know?" She gaped at him, shocked he'd figured out something she hadn't shared with another living soul.

"My wife isn't the only one with gifts, sweet girl. My brother and I are both intuitive although I seem to have the edge when it comes to you." He paused for a moment, and she sensed he was taking his time, measuring his next words carefully. "I believe he sees your mother when he looks at you, and it makes things a bit uncomfortable for him. With time, he'll see you as London and not the woman he loved so many years ago."

London felt her eyes widen in surprise, and he tilted his head to the side in silent question. "Are you not aware of how much you look like your mother? It's remarkable really—meeting you was something of a déjà vu moment for all of us."

London was speechless for several seconds. She'd always thought Asia was the one who looked the most like their mother. Before she could respond, a familiar female voice sounded from the next room.

"Unhand me, you Neanderthal. Isn't it enough you already called my brother to tattle? For Goddess sake, I wasn't going *that* fast, you are such a damned drama queen. Does your mother know you manhandle women?" Rushing around Jameson, London ran into the living room and straight into her little sister's waiting arms.

ELI LOOKED UP in time to see Trinity Frost frog-march a young woman into the living room—a woman easily identified as London's sister. He'd seen enough pictures of Paris Adler on social media to recognize her, despite her disheveled appearance. Her hair was mussed, her cheeks bright red, and she was spitting mad. Eli coughed to hide his snort of laughter when she referred to the Sheriff as a Neanderthal, but if Trin's glare was any clue, it hadn't been terribly effective. Seething, the little hellion complained about Trinity calling her brother, and Eli had to admit, the Sheriff might have crossed the line there.

"You were going ninety fucking miles per hour before you hit the city limit. What the hell were you thinking? And for your information, your brother told me to throw the book at you—seems he's tired of getting these calls. I swear to everything holy, I should paddle your ass."

If Eli hadn't been standing so close, he probably wouldn't have heard his cousin's last comment. The flair of interest in Trinity's eyes shocked Eli because the man was not usually attracted to women who didn't obey his every command, and Paris Adler seemed to be a brat of the first order. Watching the two sisters embrace, Eli felt a wash of relief coming from London he hadn't expected.

"She needed this, son. Just knowing her sister made the trip will mean a lot. And from what I've learned over the years, there is a genuine connection between sisters." Nodding, Eli reminded himself her reliance on him and on Evan would take time—that level of trust wasn't built overnight. Evan had spent a night alone with her, and tonight, Eli planned to take her back to the main house with him.

Tomorrow was going to be a big day for her—the stress of meeting with Franklin Cordesi would only be partially mitigated by Asia's presence, but tonight was his. He'd planned a romantic dinner for two on the rooftop deck. They'd be able to enjoy the night view without worrying about the temperature, thanks to the recently installed fire rail. She'd be toasty warm when he stripped her bare and fucked her until neither of them remembered their own name—he already had everything set up and was anxious to get back home with his mate.

The moon would be full in two days when they intended to claim her, but they wouldn't do it in the meadow. Instead, they would use the outdoor space they'd built atop the private wing of the mansion, saving the open field for her collaring and their official joining ceremony. He and Evan agreed it was imperative for them to know she would always hold the moment they'd made her their own close to her heart. They didn't want any embarrassment tainting what should be remembered as the most significant and intimate of their lives.

Sinking their teeth into the soft tissue where her shoulder and neck meet would send her into an immediate and cataclysmic orgasm, allowing the exchange of DNA to flow rapidly between the mates. Theirs would enable her body to heal at a greatly accelerated rate as well as improving her hearing and sense of smell. Her lifespan would be significantly increased, and she would never have to question their loyalty. Shifters mated for life—if one died, the mates would pass not long after.

Watching the two sisters speaking animatedly, their heads together as they huddled across the room, Eli found himself smiling at the obvious change in London. Looking at his dad, he shrugged. "I hadn't realized how stressed she was until now. Seeing her with her sister makes me anxious for the day she's this at ease with us all the time."

Eli didn't just want her to be relaxed with him, he wanted her to enjoy her life because, in his opinion, it didn't matter they might live for several hundred years—any time spent unhappy or unfulfilled was wasted.

"It will come, be patient with her. She's stronger than you know, but brilliant people often have highly sensitive souls. There is a vulnerability deep inside her you are charged with sheltering. London's innocence is a rare and treasured gift from the Universe, don't ever take that blessing for granted." Eli nodded his agreement. His chest felt as if someone was squeezing him from the inside out. His dad slapped him on the back and smiled.

"That pressure in your chest is love, son. It will humble you in ways you can't begin to imagine. Jack and I are always here if you need us, but for now, my advice is to get her paper sent to all the proper journals tomorrow. Enjoy all your plans, make beautiful memories, and don't let anything or anyone stand between you and your dreams."

Eli wasn't surprised his dad had picked up on what he was feeling, but his words about publishing her paper drew him up short. "What do you mean send it off tomorrow? Are you telling me she's ready to publish her findings?"

"Like all perfectionists, she will continue to recheck and cross-check until the end of time if she isn't given a small nudge." Eli understood the perils of perfectionism, he'd seen several of his friends deal with the high cost of analysis paralysis even though it had never been a problem for him.

"Why didn't I sense she was ready to publish? We could have neutralized the threat against her yesterday."

"First and foremost, she wasn't convinced it was an option until a few minutes ago. Second, you are listening on a different level than I am. Yours is every bit as important as mine—her heart needs what you'll provide tonight." His dad's words made sense, and he knew their polyamorous mating would take time to fully develop, but he wasn't happy he'd missed an opportunity to set aside the threats to his mate.

Movement across the room caught his eye and Eli watched Evan move quickly toward Trinity. *Don't worry, brother, I've got this. Take London back to the mansion through the tunnel.* Eli gave his brother a barely perceptible nod to let him know he'd heard as he watched the Sheriff's scowl turned fierce before he stalked to where London and Paris were sitting. Even at a distance, Trinity's words were crystal clear.

"Stay put until I come back for you." The look on Paris

Adler's face might have been amusing if Eli hadn't been able to see how close his friend was to losing his temper. When she started to speak Trinity growled deep in his throat. "I'm not kidding, Paris. Stay fucking put. I have a situation to deal with, and I don't want to be distracted, wondering if you're safe." Eli felt his brows raise in surprise. Hell, he'd never heard such a possessive tone from his lifelong friend. Feeling a brush of air at his side, Eli turned to see his mother smiling.

"It's about time he found her." Julia Monroe's words had barely crossed her lips when Trinity's gaze zeroed in on her.

"Don't even start, Mama J." Eli felt as if he'd walked in on a sit-com that was already in progress when his mom giggled. Trinity, along with most of their other friends, had always called Julia Mama J. Not only was she the wife of the pack's Alphas, but she was also a mother to the depths of her soul, so it was no surprise she was a favorite among the pack members, no matter their age.

"Fine. I'll stay here because I love my sister and want to make sure she is safe before I hit the road again." Paris flipped a bright pink lock of her curly hair over her shoulder and tilted her chin up in defiance—the move clearly communicating she was complying but only because she chose to. "You've already called Austin once to tattle, and he's a busy man, so there's no reason to annoy him further."

As if worrying Austin has ever been a concern for you? What the hell is this about?

Eli fought his smile as London's thoughts moved through his mind. Apparently, she'd been as surprised by

Trinity and Paris's interaction as the rest of them. As one of the pack's Alphas, Elijah wouldn't ordinarily leave without getting all the details of what caused Evan and Trinity's alarm, but the entire situation was anything but business as usual.

"Part of being an effective leader is learning to delegate, Elijah." His dad spoke from beside him, and Eli let out the breath he hadn't realized he was holding. Eli's entire life, he'd put duty above his personal needs, and he was torn between what he wanted to do and what he felt was his responsibility. "Jack and I will cover for you, and we'll keep Paris entertained until Trinity returns. Now go. Your mother wants grandchildren." Eli chuckled—he and Evan had known this was coming. The truth was their dads were the ones who were going to push for children, and everyone knew it.

Moving to stand in front of London, Eli smiled and greeted her sister, then held out his hand. "Come, Princess. It's time for us to leave." He saw her eyes widen before they dilated, and her respiration accelerated. *Perfect.*

A quick golf cart ride delivered them to the elevator leading to the private wing of the mansion he hoped they'd be sharing in the near future. Eli turned London, so she faced him, and tucked a stray lock of her hair behind her ear.

"I can't begin to tell you how much I'm looking forward to spending some alone time with you, Princess. We can do as much or as little as you like." Cupping her flushed cheek in the palm of his hand, Eli smoothed the pad of his thumb over her brow. His heart swelled when she closed her eyes, leaning into his touch. "You're like the softest kitten, pushing closer, seeking the warmth of my touch. Your sweet sighs are arrows to my heart, Princess." Eli had always been a stickler for protocol, never allowing a submissive to top from the bottom, but he found himself following her lead. Learning how to bring her pleasure was his goal, so he studied her every reaction.

He backed her into the elevator when the doors finally slid open, appreciating the catch in her breath when her back pressed against the cool mirrored wall. "You smell amazing." He nuzzled the soft skin below her ear, inhaling her scent, letting it seep into his soul. When the elevator pinged past the floor where she and Evan had exited, he felt her tense. "We're going up to the roof, Princess. I have a surprise for you."

Chapter Eighteen

L ONDON'S HEAD WAS spinning as the door of the elevator slid open, revealing a breathtaking rooftop terrace. It was easy to get caught up in the wonder of the Monroe brothers. The sensual spell they wove around her was as dizzying as the rapid ascent to this rooftop paradise. She gasped as she took in her surroundings, the enormous outdoor living space obviously not something she'd expected to find on top of Eli's home. *It's more than I could have ever imagined. It's like being transported to a tropical resort without having to endure airport security checkpoints or crowded travel packed into a flying can-like sardine.* Eli smiled to himself, knowing she had only to ask her brother for the use of the Adler Oil jet, but he doubted she'd ever done so.

Palm trees in huge pots lined the edge of the covered area, and he could hear her silent questions about how much longer they'd be left outside. Fresh flowers cascaded from hanging baskets and decorated numerous tabletops as flickering candles gave the area a glow despite the shade from the cover overhead. Outdoor heaters hummed nearby, and she smiled, thanking him for his thoughtfulness.

"I'm speechless, Elijah. It's amazing. You've gone to an

incredible amount of work, and I want you to know how much I appreciate it."

"You're welcome, Princess. We don't usually have the opportunity to enjoy this space this late in the season. I'm thrilled we've gotten this one last chance." Pulling her into his arms, Eli watched her eyes flare with desire as he erased the last few inches separating them. Pressing his lips against hers, he savored the sweet taste and happily accepted her invitation for more when she parted her lips beneath his. Exploring every inch of her mouth, Eli cradled the back of her head in his large hand. Seconds later, he fisted his hand in her hair, tilting her head to give him better access. Deepening the kiss, he felt the first stirrings of his change and had to focus on holding back his wolf.

She must have sensed his momentary distraction because she broke their kiss and stared into his eyes. "Your eyes are glimmering with golden highlights. Does that happen before you shift? Will you show me?"

He was surprised by her request but shouldn't have been. His little mate was inquisitive by nature—her insatiable quest for knowledge would serve the scientific community well. Eli knew there were numerous medical issues the shifter community was facing, and he hoped, at some point, she'd be able to lend her expertise to the discussions.

Without responding, he stepped back and started un-buttoning his shirt. "This isn't the way I saw things playing out, Princess." He flashed her a wicked grin as he tossed the soft cotton garment aside. "I'd planned to get you naked first, but I'm not ashamed of who I am, and you deserve to see what you're getting in to." Without saying anything more, he removed the rest of his clothing, then let his wolf take over. She watched in wide-eyed fascination as his body morphed into his wolf form. When the transition was complete, she knelt beside him with her hand extended and upturned. Closing the distance between them, he pressed the side of his face against her hand.

"You're so beautiful. I had no idea." She ran her hand through his coat, and Eli would have growled in appreciation if he hadn't been worried the deep sound might frighten her. "You're so much larger than a regular wolf, I can see why there have been occasional reports of larger wolves around the country. I'm in awe… really, I'm having trouble processing it all at once. I'll probably pester you for hours with questions, but I swear none of them will ever be meant as a judgment."

Licking her hand, he smiled to himself when she giggled.

"Oh, my. I am imagining a lot of wonderful uses for your wicked tongue." He nudged the end of his snout between her legs and inhaled. Growling his approval, he moved his long nose under the hem of her dress and yipped with happiness when her sweet cream glistened in the dark. Pushing his nose against the swollen lips of her pussy, Eli was grateful they'd forbidden her to wear panties. It was tempting to lap her sweet cream with slow swipes of his tongue, but he'd save that pleasure for later. He wanted to tie her to him with pleasure, but he knew being in his human form would make communication easier. Eli could already feel their love building. Trust would come over time, but for now, he could give her the pleasure her body craved.

When her legs began to tremble, he stepped back. Shifting back into his human form, Eli stood to his full height, crossing his muscular arms over his bare chest, watching her eyes move over him in an intimate caress so hot, he felt his cock twitch.

"Damn. Your body is the stuff of fantasies." London had spoken more about him than to him, but Eli didn't mind—knowing she appreciated his body fed his ego as no other woman could.

"I'm glad you approve. Now, I want you naked, Princess." His words didn't seem to register, giving him insight into how she'd be when she was working. It would be fun to approach his sweet mate in her lab and see if he couldn't distract her. "Now, London. Strip." The sharp tone of his voice, combined with the compelling undertone of being an Alpha, broke the spell, and she quickly pulled the dress over her head. "You are stunning—literally a fucking work of art." He saw doubt clouding her eyes and shook his head.

"Don't you dare say anything negative about yourself. The only spanking I want to give you tonight is one that brings you pleasure." Her eyes widened, and he smiled. "Oh yes, sweet mate. I'm going to turn your delectable ass a lovely shade of deep rose—you'll be lifting into the swats, begging to come." She didn't look at all convinced, but she'd soon learn he meant what he said. Eli held out his hand and was pleased when she placed hers atop his without hesitation.

"Let's play a bit, then we'll eat." He saw her eyes dart from side to side and shook his head. "We don't need clothes. Shifters are very comfortable with their bodies. My brother and I want you to start becoming at ease with your nudity because we plan to keep you bared to our gaze and touch as often as possible."

Pulling her close, he sealed his lips over hers, savoring the sweet flavor he'd come to associate with his mate. Lifting her into his arms without breaking the kiss, Eli moved to an oversized lounger close to one of the overhead heaters.

"It feels like we're enjoying a warm day at the beach... although I have to admit, I've never skinny dipped."

"Oh, Princess, we will remedy that as soon as possible. We have a lovely lake on pack land, and of course, there is always the pool. Watching you swim naked will probably become one of my favorite ways to spend a summer afternoon." Lifting her left ankle, he moved it to the corner of the lounger and secured it with a Velcro strap. Repeating the process on her right side, he moved up and held his hand out. "Give me your wrist, London."

Once she was secured, he stood at the end of the well-padded chair and watched her for any signs of extreme fear or discomfort. She tugged at the restraints, testing them, but didn't appear frightened, so he was calling it a win.

"I'm going to explore every inch of you. I want to know what makes you sigh and what floods your lovely pussy with sweet cream." He'd been moving his eyes over her, watching all her physiological responses but returned his gaze to hers before continuing. "What are your safe words, London?" She bit her lower lip, a fleeting look of trepidation flickering in her eyes before she won whatever internal battle she'd waged and nodded.

"Yellow for a time out and red if I am past what I can

endure physically or emotionally."

"Perfect. Don't forget them. I prefer you use yellow so we can preempt anything more upsetting, but never forget they are both available. I'll be studying you carefully, but tonight is all about pleasure. I don't anticipate you will need either of them, but there are times you may encounter triggers even you may not know are a problem." Giving her several seconds to process what he'd said, he deliberately softened his expression before continuing.

"You are a dream come true, Princess... the answer to a thousand whispered prayers." She didn't know it now, but she would be the most cherished woman in the world. Not only would Eli and Evan wrap the moon in silk for her, the rest of their pack members would lay down their lives for her as well.

Grabbing a silk scarf from a nearby table, he covered her eyes and smiled when he saw her pulse accelerate. "Tell me what you're thinking, Princess."

"It's scary, but not frightening... exciting without being overwhelming. I can feel the heat radiating deep into my muscles, relaxing me despite my anticipation." Her answer was so much more than he could have asked for, and he suspected she was one of those rare treasures who found freedom in bondage and being blindfolded. She was in a word—perfect.

Elijah spent the next half hour mapping every inch of his mate's body—kissing, licking, and nipping—to see which sensations she loved and making a note of any she didn't appreciate. By the time he'd finished with her front, she was moaning his name and trying to lift her hips. Eli couldn't wait to tie her to the medical table in their dungeon. He and Evan could spend hours bringing her to the brink of release before backing off. Orgasm denial was one of his favorite forms of punishment—he found it much more effective than spanking.

"Knowing I get to fuck you with nothing between us is making me insane, Princess. I can hardly wait to push my aching cock between your slick folds. The addictive scent of your swollen pussy is etched into my soul."

"Please. Oh God, please fuck me." Hearing her beg was the sweetest sound in the world. Quick gasping breaths, the rapid rise and fall of her chest highlighted by the pink blush of arousal—hell, everything about London flipped his switches. He'd played with submissives at clubs all over the world, but none of them held a candle to the beauty spread out before him.

"I'd planned to explore the other side before taking you, Princess, but I can't wait." Moving over her, he drew the tip of his throbbing cock through her drenched folds and groaned. "Fuck, you are so wet for me. Do you have any idea what a turn on that is?"

"I want to touch you." Her plea was spoken like the most reverent prayer, but he didn't dare untie her.

"Not this time, *Amore Mio*." It settled something inside him to admit it—London was his love. He didn't remember all the Italian he'd learned in college, but it pleased him to realize he'd retained what was important. "My control is tenuous at best; your soft fingers would be too much for me to endure. I want this to last as long as possible, and you have to come at least twice before I let go." Pushing in a few inches, he groaned. "So. Fucking. Tight."

He pushed the rigid ring surrounding the purple head

of his cock inside and waited while her vaginal muscles fluttered around him. Eli's corona was ultra-sensitive, so he sucked in a deep breath to push back the blinding urge to shove himself balls deep. *More. Oh, please. More.* Hearing her thoughts was such an incredible level of intimacy, Eli thought his heart would burst. *I want you both... I want to know what it's like to be fucked by two men at once. I need to know if I can be what you need.*

Her internal dialogue felt like a punch to the gut. Eli had no idea London doubted her ability to be what he and his brother wanted. Hell, he'd been focused on proving they were worthy, he hadn't stopped to consider she might be worrying about the same thing. Sending a quick telepathic message to his brother, he refocused his attention on the remarkable woman beneath him. Rolling one of her peaked nipples between his finger and thumb, Eli gave the puckered nub a quick pinch, then groaned when she went liquid around him.

"You are so responsive, Princess. Fucking perfect. Listen to my voice and come when I give the command." Setting a quick pace that had him gaining a fraction of an inch with each thrust, he fought the urge to ravage her when he felt her muscles contracting around him before he was fully seated. "Not yet, London. Hold it a few seconds longer. Your orgasm will be so much stronger if you delay it as long as you can." His warning was met with a warm rush of her cream coating his cock and making it easier to press forward the last couple of inches. When he felt his tip nudge against her cervix, Eli set his jaw and commanded, "Now, London. Come for me. Give me your pleasure."

Riding out the storm of her release was the sweetest

torture in the world. The strength of her contractions was easier to endure after he'd slipped the blindfold from her eyes. Looking into the fathomless blue depths was like falling into the Caribbean Sea—the intensity of the blue deceptive, the surroundings warm and inviting. *Distracting.* He waited until the contractions eased, then pinched her clit sending her ass over tea-kettle into another release.

"That's a good girl. Milk me, Princess. Fucking hell, you are temptation personified." He groaned and started mentally reviewing the pack's latest financials in an attempt to hold off his own release. *I warned you.* Evan's voice echoed through Eli's mind, and he was grateful for the distraction. "Okay, *Amore Mio,* one more, and this time, I want you to take me with you." Pulling back until only the very tip of his cock remained inside, Eli rocked his hips forward, using the rigid corona to stimulate her G-spot before thrusting deep. Repeating the move, again and again, he felt her vagina flood and knew she was close.

"Oh God. I'm going to come, Eli... Sir." The words were music to his ears—knowing she was trying to learn protocol snapped the last threads of his control. Thrusting hard and fast, Eli followed her over the edge. Fireworks exploded behind his eyelids, and electricity sparked in every cell in his body, frying his brain for several long seconds as his seed pulsed deep inside the woman he planned to spend the rest of his life with.

"I'll undo the bindings as soon as I'm able to move, Princess. Fucking hell, I think you toasted my brain and smoked my muscles." The muscles in his arms quivered under the continued strain, and he sent up a silent prayer he wouldn't collapse on top of her. Pulling in a deep breath, he let the infusion of oxygen work its miracle. When his brain fog cleared, Eli moved to the side before releasing her arms and legs. Pulling her against his chest, Eli rolled them both to the side, tucking her head under his chin.

"My fantasies about what it would be like to make love to you out in the open didn't hold a candle to the real thing." He'd fucked her the day before, but this had been so much more. "I've been dreaming about finding my mate since I first shifted, but you are the answer to my deepest desires—proof the Universe rewards those who are persistent and patient."

"I was too young when Austin, Bronx, and Cleveland hit puberty to understand all the chatter about shifting. My young mind assumed everyone was talking about the hormonal changes every young man experiences. By the time Israel and Kensington made the transition, my parents would have known enough about my inquisitive nature to make certain I was kept out of the loop."

He chuckled at the admission. He could well imagine any parent attempting to avoid the inquisition of a brilliant child. Everything he'd learned about her, including conversations with several of her siblings, confirmed London's quest for information had always been unquenchable. Almost every one of her nine siblings had cautioned him to remember London's brilliance in the lab came at a high cost—she'd missed a lot of the social experiences most women her age take for granted.

Elijah had promised London's family her heart was safe in their care, and he'd been relieved to know none of them had seemed alarmed about her involvement in a polyamorous relationship. The only Adler sibling whose response had surprised him was Kensington. It appeared the man, who was world famous for his sex-on-a-stick roles, was fiercely protective of his younger sister's heart.

Several of the female members of the pack had been more than happy to sing the man's praises when he'd asked them about Kensington. Since the entertainment industry wasn't Eli's area of expertise, he'd decided to take them at their word rather than researching the man's movie roles. For a man involved in one of the most liberal industries on the planet, Kensington Adler was remarkably traditional in his views of love and commitment.

Eli brushed a stray curl from the side of London's face and pressed a kiss against her forehead. "I've talked to all of your siblings, Princess, and only one threatened to rip my throat out if I ever made you cry."

"Kensington." It hadn't been a question, and a ghost of a smile twitched at the corners of her lush lips. "He's a trip, isn't he? It always surprises people when they figure out how traditional he is." She rolled to her back and seemed to be searching the first twinkling stars for her next words.

"I know everyone expects Austin to be overly protective, and he can be. But it's Kenz who comes at you from left field. People assume he is some super-liberal, metro-male because he's an actor, but he's always been my champion. He's the one who beat up the bullies on the playground who teased me about being a geek. And he was the one who flew across the country to escort me to my last sorority formal."

A single tear slipped from the corner of her eye before disappearing into her dark hair, and Eli felt a tidal wave of emotion wash over him. Knowing the story she was telling him was monumentally important to her was the only thing keeping him from pulling her into his arms and kissing the pain away.

"Paris called him… she can't keep a secret to save her. She knew my date had dumped me for one of the new pledges. Honestly, I wouldn't have cared if it hadn't been the last formal dance of my college career, meaning I was obligated to attend. Worse yet, I knew photographs from the entire soiree would be plastered all over social media. Just thinking about the embarrassment of standing out like a sore thumb without a date, ridiculed on hundreds of internet posts was overwhelming." She paused for so long, he wasn't sure whether or not she would finish her story. Finally, after several deep breaths, she turned to him and gave him a wan smile.

"Kenz had flowers… lots and lots of flowers… delivered to my sorority house. When the arrangements overwhelmed my room, we started filling the downstairs reception and living areas. It was so over-the-top, and typical Kenz, all I could do was laugh, and I'm sure that was exactly what he intended. Well, that and he was making a statement. Big brother didn't want any of the women he referred to as snobs questioning how important I was to him. The last delivery was a dozen red roses in a Lalique Champs-Elysees Vase." He must have looked confused because she laughed and nodded her head.

"I know. I know. Don't feel bad, I was clueless too, but one of my mega-wealthy sorority sisters knew, and she didn't waste any time telling everybody who would listen the pretty piece of glass as they'd referred to it was, in fact, a six-thousand-dollar treasure."

"I'll bet the House Mother was in a panic." Holy shit, who sends a vase that valuable to a college sorority house?

"Oh, yes indeed. She'd already been in a tizzy about the flowers covering every horizontal surface, but I thought she was going to launch into space over a six-grand vase. Then she practically fainted into a heap when she opened the front door, and Kensington walked in. Every card contained a clue, and I'd figured out he was coming before the fifth delivery. I was ready and waiting for him downstairs... A good thing too, I kept him from being mobbed." *Well, mostly.*

Eli grinned at her and thanked the Great Goddess for sending him a mate who wasn't just brilliant and beautiful but also enchanting company. The conversation between them flowed effortlessly as they laid side-by-side, laughing about how her brother had disrupted the formal dance. The date who'd stood her up got a quick lesson in karma when his own date fawned over Kensington all evening. London hadn't gloated when she'd shared that piece of the story, merely said she hoped he'd learned a valuable lesson, so he didn't make the same mistake again. Eli vowed he would spend the rest of his life sheltering her kind heart.

Chapter Nineteen

E VAN SHOULD HAVE been dead on his feet. He'd been in surgery for ten hours, piecing together the bone fragments of a young woman's shattered leg. The car she'd been riding in was broadsided by a drunk driver, and the truth was, she was damned lucky to be alive. She faced a significant amount of rehabilitation, but she didn't appear to have any head or internal injuries.

Orthopedic surgery was his specialty, but if the young lady hadn't been a member of his pack, he might have transferred her to a larger facility with a team of surgeons. Her time on the table would have been significantly reduced, and the margin for error would have been slashed to near zero. But as a shifter, there would have been questions her family found difficult to answer. Hell, her body had already begun mending and rebuilding the bone before he'd finished closing the eight-inch incision. Evan hadn't bothered with sutures—unnecessary with the speed with which she would heal. After a long shower, he'd checked in on her and was pleased to see the skin had already fused and the scar disappearing quickly.

Blocking the erotic pictures his brother and their mate had been unconsciously sending had taken considerable effort, but he hadn't needed or wanted the distraction. His patient was resting comfortably now, left in capable hands with instructions to call if there was any change. He didn't plan to keep his phone on him once he joined London and Eli, but he'd worked out a signal with Seth. If Evan was needed, the lights in the master suite and the roof terrace would begin flashing.

He also directed the clinic's human resources director to begin searching for additional staff. Evan knew he'd been stalling. Adding physicians and support staff in any medical facility was an enormous undertaking, but a selective search in the shifter community added another layer of difficulty. He'd been dreading the arduous task of interviewing, reviewing background checks, and training. Until London came into his life, he hadn't cared it was consumed with work. Now, Evan wanted the opportunity to build a life centered around his mate. Even though he and Eli would work together, they were both going to need to cut their work schedules back significantly.

Leaving his phone on the dresser in the master suite, Evan made his way to the rooftop terrace. Stepping off the elevator, the sight greeting him was straight out of every Dom's favorite fantasy. London kneeling on a pillow, her pussy exposed, the drenched folds of her labia glistening in the candlelight stole his breath. Hell, it was all he could do to step off the elevator without stumbling over his own feet.

"It appears your other Master has arrived, Princess. Tell him what your heart desires."

Evan shot his brother a questioning look, relieved at the sparkle he saw in Eli's bright green eyes. Maybe *I shouldn't have blocked you so effectively—but fuck me six ways to Tuesday, brother, you were killing me.* Evan felt his brother's amusement even though his expression never changed.

Her form isn't perfect, but her heart is pure—the desire to please nothing but sincere. Evan acknowledged Eli's message with a quick nod.

"I want to see if I can be what you want. I mean, I want to try ménage so we all know if I can do it. And if you'll let me keep working, I'd like to stay and see if we…I mean, I… shit, I'm messing this up." Evan moved closer, kneeling in front of her. Tilting her chin up with his fingers, he shook his head.

"No, baby, you are doing fine. Speaking from your heart is never a mistake. When the elevator doors opened, I was so overwhelmed by the vision of you presenting yourself to me, I could barely breathe." Smoothing her hair back, Evan took in her luminous eyes and felt like his heart was expanding out of his chest.

"Let us claim you tonight, baby. Belong to us. You are everything we've dreamed of finding. We'll stand at your side and help you make all your dreams come true."

"Our amazing mate has been wearing larger and larger plugs for the past several hours. She's ready." Eli words were a welcome relief, but ready physically didn't necessarily mean she was ready emotionally for the changes her body was going to undergo.

She knows but isn't sure we know what we're getting into. She is amazing. We will work on her confidence, brother.

"We're going to make you our own, baby. I only have one request—I want to see the feisty woman who stood up to me outside her sister's room. That beautiful, take-charge spitfire rocked my world, and I know she's still in there somewhere." He tapped his finger against her nose and grinned when her.

"It's been a long few weeks. I hate how this has burned me out. I'm going to submit my paper first thing in the morning. Living in fear for myself was hard enough, but knowing I'm endangering you, your family, friends, and the members of your pack… well, it's just too much." Evan agreed, it was too much for anyone to deal with alone. He vowed to make it a priority to prove to her that she would never again face adversity without them at her side.

"I could promise you facing the world alone is in your past, but I know it would be little more than sweet words until you see it for yourself." Pulling her up with him, he wrapped his arms around her, hoping she'd absorb a fraction of the love he felt for her. "Give yourself to us tonight, London. We'll make certain you never regret the decision."

She didn't move out of his arms to respond, but he felt her body relax against his. Her whispered "Yes" would have been inaudible to anyone other than a shifter, but the single word reverberated to the depths of his soul. He scooped her up into his arms and moved to the oversized lounger near one of the outdoor heaters. They'd still be under the stars, but he wouldn't worry about her becoming chilled before they claimed her. Once their DNA entered her system, she'd have a virtually unlimited ability to tolerate the cold, but for now, it was important she was comfortable.

Evan didn't waste any time stripping and laying down beside her. "Come here, baby." Eli helped her move into position, then Evan lifted her until the tip of his cock was poised at her entrance. "Ride me, London. Take your pleasure." He wanted her to come as quickly as she could and preferably more than once. Her eyes widened in surprise, but she didn't hesitate to sink down until he felt the sensitive tip of his cock pressing against her cervix.

Pleased to see his sweet mate was already regaining some of the weight she'd lost over the past few months, Evan skimmed his hands over her breasts. The glow in her cheeks and fading dark circles under her eyes made him grateful they'd been working hard to make certain she ate right and was getting plenty of sleep. It hadn't taken them long to discover she seemed to rest best nestled between them—certainly not a hardship for Eli or him.

"Fuck me, baby. You are so tight with the plug. Your vaginal muscles are already flexing around me, trying to hold me deep—when I have no intention of leaving." This time was all about her. Her pace. Her pleasure.

ELIJAH WATCHED AS the woman he would claim as his mate rode his brother. For the first time, he was able to watch from a distance, lost in her pleasure, screaming Evan's name as she flew over the edge in an orgasm he suspected had blindsided her. Evan pulled her against his chest, running his hands in soothing sweeps up and down the length of her spine.

Eli eased onto the lounger behind her, grateful he'd already removed the robe he wore. The lube he'd warmed earlier slid down the crack of her ass without London seeming to notice—perfect. He didn't want to shatter the sated bliss she was enjoying, but he needed to take advantage of her relaxed state to prepare her for their dual possession.

Removing the plug in one fluid motion drew a low moan from London, but he was pleased when she didn't make any effort to shift positions. Rolling a condom over his erection, he used a generous amount of warm lube, then began pressing himself against her rear hole. Eli gripped her hips as Evan wrapped his arms around her when she tried to press back seeking more.

"Hold still, Princess, we're going to take this nice and slow. Our pace, not yours."

"No torn tissues, baby. We want you to enjoy this as much as we're going to."

Eli could feel Evan's concern and sent him a silent affirmation he was determined to make this experience one London would remember fondly for the rest of her life. Advancing with slow, short strokes, pushing through the tight ring of muscles of her anus, Eli let out a breath he hadn't known he was holding.

"Fucking hell, Princess, you're killing me. You are perfect. Come when you're ready." Ideally, they'd claim her during a release. Biting into the tender flesh where her shoulder joined her neck during her orgasm was the best possible scenario. The increased blood flow would pump the healing properties of their DNA through her system at an accelerated rate, keeping any pain she felt from the punctures in her skin to a minimum, and hopefully, flooding her system with endorphins would blur the line between pleasure and pain.

With a silent nod, indicating he was ready, Eli felt Evan lift London until his cock slid almost all the way from her channel. Pushing forward, Eli let Evan set the pace since his brother was the one who could see London's face and read her expressions. They'd only completed three thrusts when he felt her tremble between them. Her entire body clenched, forcing Eli to tighten his jaw to stave off his own release. *Fucking hell, she is killing me.*

Opening his eyes, he saw Evan's mouth open over her left shoulder. Telling himself to focus on the woman between them and not his own needs, he gave Evan a quick nod. Leaning close, he opened his mouth, grateful his body had been better prepared than his mind since his incisors were already fully elongated. Still in the throes of orgasm, London screamed as their sharp teeth punctured her tender skin, but the euphoric feeling their saliva carried into her bloodstream washed away the initial pain in seconds. Her scream filled the air, and Eli knew it would be heard for miles around. Any pack members outside running would know their Alphas had just claimed their mate.

London's earth-shattering release triggered Eli's, and he heard his brother shout her name at the same time. The lights exploding behind his eyelids were a testament to the bone-melting pleasure of coming inside her tight ass. He felt the moment their three souls fused as one and wondered if he looked as changed on the outside as he felt on the inside. Licking the puncture wounds, he watched in wonder as they sealed. Any other scars she had would be erased, but the two holes from each of her mates would always remain faintly visible as a sign to the world she'd been claimed.

"My entire body is tingling. It's the strangest thing ever."

London was trying to push herself up from where she'd been sprawled over Evan's chest, but he only allowed her to shift her position enough to give Eli room to clean and dry her. Once he was satisfied the tender tissues wouldn't chafe, Eli grabbed a blanket from a nearby warmer. Wrapping it around her, he lifted her into his arms. Leaning against the back of the lounger, Eli helped Evan drape London's legs over his lap so they were both able to maintain the skin to skin contact that would further strengthen their union.

"Talk to us, baby. What are you feeling?" Evan's hands were stroking up and back down her legs, the movement seemed to soothe any lingering physical discomfort she was experiencing. Eli could feel the muscles in London's back and shoulders slowly draining of tension as he mirrored his brother's movements.

"The strange tingly feeling is fading, but I still feel like there is an intense heat coursing through my entire body. I know you said your DNA would alter my system, but I guess I didn't think about how those changes might *feel.*" Eli smiled as he watched her struggle to process everything she was feeling. "It's so strange to not have the words to describe something. I've spent most of my life describing the problems I wanted to solve and the discoveries I made along the way. But this... this is something so different. It's so deeply personal, and I feel altered in ways I can't describe." She shook her head as if trying to clear the fog, but he could tell her it would take several days for all the sensations to settle.

"Princess, everything you are experiencing is normal. It will take a while for your body to adjust."

"We'll answer any questions we can. If you have concerns we can't address, we'll find a resource for you. There are dozens of pack members who will be thrilled to help. The important thing is that you ask." Eli nodded in agreement—good communication would make or break their union.

"No question is too personal or insignificant. You didn't get to be one of the most recognized names in research by shying away from asking questions, Princess—apply that same tenacious curiosity here." He felt the shift in her, the understanding and acceptance of what he'd just said.

"It's going to take me a little while to sort through everything. And I want to get my paper sent off as soon as possible. I'm not naïve enough to think it will neutralize the threats entirely, but it should help."

Evan had already explained the process to Eli. London would be called to defend her findings and consult with anyone hired to verify her findings. Eli didn't claim to understand the process. The insanity of her being required to help those trying to disprove her findings was something he was still trying to wrap his head around.

"Seeing Paris today makes me wonder how long until more of my siblings make a sudden appearance." Sighing, she shook her head. "I have to admit, Asia is the one I expected to show up. Brooklyn is working full-time trying to get her consulting business off the ground. Catalina is on the other side of the planet most of the time—personally, I think she is running from her attraction to Cooper Hicks." Eli and Evan chuckled because they agreed the pair seemed to have a love-hate relationship that challenged them both.

"Paris graduates next Spring, and I just realized I don't know what she plans to do after that. Geez, I'm the worst sister ever. I've been so caught up in my work, I've only seen two of my siblings since Brooklyn was shot… and one of those was work-related."

Eli hoped she'd be able to cut back her work hours in the near future—having her lab in a secured location and submitting her research for publication should help alleviate some of the pressure she'd been under.

LONDON WAS STILL reeling from the aftershocks of the most explosive orgasm of her life. The tingling sensation racing through her blood was the weirdest thing she'd ever experienced. She found herself struggling to focus because there was suddenly so much background noise. Eli and Evan encouraged her to ask questions but struggling with the sensory overload made it difficult to put her thoughts into words. When she'd mentioned being surprised Asia hadn't been the one to show up, Eli had stiffened beneath her, and Evan's cheeks flushed.

"Asia is here, baby. She flew in earlier today, but we asked her to hold off until tomorrow morning to give you and Eli time alone."

It would probably surprise them, but she appreciated them stalling her big sister's visit. London loved Asia with all her heart, but her oldest sister could be damned intimidating.

"She will be arriving with Franklin Cordesi." London felt her mouth fall open, but before she could ask the obvious question, Evan held up his hand and looked to Eli.

"I'm not sure exactly how this has all come down, but I find it reassuring to know you'll have an additional advocate in the room." They'd already arranged for Trinity to be onsite, and he'd promised to drive Paris back to the mansion if she decided to return to town rather than staying the night at Evan's. The Sheriff had growled that Paris was a hazard on the road, but she'd waved him off, insisting he had a stick up his ass. If you asked London, their interaction looked a lot like Catalina and Cooper's. *If he thinks Paris drives too fast, he'll have a stroke when he meets Cleveland.*

"Let's get you downstairs and into bed. You have a full day ahead of you tomorrow and being well rested will help. Running on fumes for so long takes a toll, and you need to spend some time recovering."

Nodding, she let them lead her downstairs. Standing in front of the en suite's mirror, London stared at a woman who looked only vaguely familiar. The haunted eyes she'd been sporting when Evan first rescued her looked clearer, the dark circles fading quickly.

Don't ever underestimate the power of love, sweetheart... it heals from the inside out.

London heard her mother's voice so clearly, it was almost as if she was in the room. Sucking in a quick breath, she gripped the edge of the marble when her knees threatened to fold out from under her. Strong hands gripped her shoulders, holding her steady.

"Are you okay, baby?"

Evan's gaze was locked on hers in the mirror, and she felt a rush of relief knowing he'd sensed her distress and rushed to check on her. Tears overflowed her eyes, leaving silver trails down her cheeks. She had no idea why she was so emotional, the over-the-top response was unusual for her. *Well, hearing your mom's voice wasn't exactly business as usual.*

"You may be experiencing a delayed adrenaline crash, but I have the feeling it's something more. Talk to me, love."

"I heard my mom's voice. Looking in the mirror, noting I look… I don't know… healthier, I heard her say love heals from the inside out." Evan turned her, pulling her against his chest, and London relished how perfect it felt to be pressed against his heart. Letting his calm wash over her, London wondered why she'd refused to return his calls. Her only explanation was he'd seemed so confident, so self-assured, for the first time in her life, she'd been both attracted to and terrified of a man.

"Remember, your senses are going to be greatly enhanced. Your hearing and night vision will likely be the first changes you notice."

She nodded her understanding even though she knew hearing her mom had been different. The experience had blindsided her, and London wasn't sure where the sound had come from. In some ways, it seemed as if the words had merely echoed in her mind, but they'd seemed so real, she caught herself searching the room… expecting to see her mom standing nearby.

Lead with your heart, darling girl. Open yourself up to the gifts the Goddess bestows on you. The Universe doesn't reward those who are not worthy. Your brilliance is going to change the world—let your special gifts make their own changes.

Safe in Evan's arms, London let a familiar voice comfort rather than startle her, and for the first time in years, she realized it was okay to rely on someone else.

Chapter Twenty

A SIA SEETHED IN the passenger seat as Franklin drove to what Eli Monroe referred to as the main house. She should be happy as a clam; the conversation she'd had with Austin early this morning had been damned entertaining. Knowing big brother's assistant had surprised him should have had her dancing for joy, but her own sexual frustration cast a pall over everything. She was pissy, and it wasn't a good look for her.

"Would you care to explain your attitude, *Cara*?" The low pitch of his voice was deliberate, forcing her to pay close attention in order to hear him. Who did he think he was dealing with? A fucking amateur who didn't recognize manipulation?

"I'm not your *dear.*" *As evidenced by the cold shoulder brush off you gave me last night after dinner.* He'd flirted with her, but then he'd pressed a chaste kiss to her forehead and walked away. Why did he bother with adjoining rooms if he wasn't interested? It didn't make any sense, and if she was honest with herself, her ego was badly bruised by the brush off.

"I'm fine. How much longer until we find this place?" She'd been annoyed when he held out his hand for her car keys. Damn it, she'd rented a sporty car because she loved the maneuverability on the curvy roads in the northeast. Hell, it didn't matter what you drove outside Austin, most of the roads she used were flat and endless.

"My sisters taught me at an early age the words *I'm fine* are the most dangerous words a woman can utter." Turning to look at him, she was surprised to see a rakish smile she hadn't seen before. "Did you know London submitted her research to a number of publications this morning? And I believe Ian McGregor is coordinating a press release as we speak."

His abrupt change of subject threw her for a few seconds, but she recovered quickly. Damn it all to hell, she wasn't going to be thrown off her game by this man. *I'm not losing this damned game. You want to play with the big girls? Batter up, baby.* Watching as he turned, slowing to a stop in front of a massive gate, she held off her response until they'd been granted entrance.

"Yes. I got a message from her this morning, but I'm worried it may not be enough to keep her safe."

"The Consortium will not be easily dissuaded. Her testimony would be damning, so they will want to minimize any potential damage."

"And it would be much easier to convince the public London's findings are flawed if she's unable to defend her research, correct?" He nodded, confirming her suspicions. Surprising her once again, he pulled to the side of the gravel drive and turned to her.

"You and London look a lot alike at a distance. I want you to be careful, *Cara.*"

"I'm taller, and we don't dress anything alike. I can't imagine anyone mistaking us." *He's lost his damned mind.*

Their hair color wasn't even the same. London's long curly blonde hair and sparkling blue eyes made her stand out in a crowd even when she wore the damned lab coats she always seemed to be hiding in.

"The technology snipers use involves facial recognition, *Cara*."

He was starting to really annoy her with that sappy nickname. If he thought she was so fucking dear, why did he leave her hanging last night? Damn it all to hell, she'd been forced to break out her trusty traveling companion to take the edge off. Thank the Goddess for her battery-operated boyfriend. Her bruised ego was still smarting from Franklin's rejection.

"They will believe the computer before they give a second thought to things so easily changed—hair color, clothing, sexy shoes." She watched his eyes darken as his gaze moved down the length of her leg to take in her black leather stiletto boots. She felt the heat of his appreciative look as his eyes seemed to retrace their way back up until he met her gaze.

"Just be aware of your surroundings, Asia. I believe your younger sister could also be in danger, and I suspect she will be less self-aware. Paris will take her cues from you—if you act concerned and exercise caution, perhaps she'll be more inclined to be careful as well."

The rat bastard played her perfectly. Cordesi had to know she would do anything to protect her sisters, and if that meant pretending to be paranoid, then so be it. Fuck a famous fairy, she hated knowing she'd been played.

When they parked in front of the largest home Asia had ever seen, she couldn't stop staring at the massive structure. "Holy shit. This is where Elijah Monroe lives?"

"I'm under the impression it's more than a single-family home." He laid his hand on her thigh when she reached for the door handle and shook his head. "Wait until I come around, *Cara*." The words had been gently spoken, but there was no question they represented a command. His mercurial approach to her was setting a lightning pace to move from annoying to infuriating.

Making their way up the sweeping staircase, Asia was startled when the front door flew open, crashing into the inside wall as London stood a few feet in front of her, all color drained from her pale face. Before Asia could put words to her surprise, Franklyn lifted her into his arms and sprinted up the last few steps. A man who looked a lot like Dr. Evan Monroe wrapped his arms around London, lifting her feet from the floor before moving her away from the entrance.

Before Franklin was able to carry her past the threshold, the silence around them was shattered by what sounded like a rifle shot echoing off the stone walls of the portico. Franklin jerked but didn't drop her even as his steps faltered. The door slammed closed behind them, and Franklin gently set her on her feet, sucking in a deep breath and sagging against the wall. Phones were ringing all around her, but it all faded to background noise as Asia focused on the blood smear beside Franklin's shoulder.

"We've got him." The sharp voice came over the radio on the belt of a huge man standing nearby, pulling Asia out of her stunned silence.

"Franklin's hurt." Asia heard the panic in her voice as she grabbed his uninjured arm to help him stand up straight and move further into the enormous home. Evan stepped in to take her place, but she directed him to the other side. Seating Franklin on one of the barstools lining the largest kitchen island Asia had ever seen, she stood by helplessly as Evan cut away the sleeves of Franklin's ruined leather jacket and linen shirt.

Taking the damp cloth one of the kitchen staff held out to him, Evan cleaned the slash before frowning. "Not as bad as I thought, but it definitely needs stitches." Asia felt herself sway in response to the bloody visual. Fuck a duck, she'd never been able to stand the sight of blood. London wrapped an arm around her, leading her to a nearby chair.

"I saw it... I was coming down the stairs, and it played out in my mind like one of those old-time movies they used to play in the park when we were kids. But then I opened the door, and you were fine... so I thought I'd imagined it." London turned to smile her thanks to the young woman who set an engraved silver tray complete with steaming cups of coffee and cookies on the table beside her. Asia lifted one of the pretty china cups, amazed at how delicate the rose-covered piece of history looked in her hand. Inhaling, the smell of the freshly brewed elixir of life teased her nostrils and calmed her in the way nothing else could.

Asia started to stand when Evan began leading Franklin from the room, but London grasped her upper arm and shook her head. "We'll catch up with them in a few minutes. Let Evan get him stitched up first. They're going to take the elevator down to the tunnel and use a cart to transport him to the clinic." Asia stared at her sister in stunned silence. "It will be safer than taking him out the front and driving around. Much faster as well." London's grin helped diffuse some of the tension surrounding them.

The two sisters chatted for several minutes before Paris burst into the room, squealing with delight to find them downing their second cup of coffee.

"In the name of all things sacred, please tell me there's more. I think you have to have a tech degree to operate Evan's coffee maker, good grief." Thanking the young woman who delivered another tray, the three sisters busied themselves sharing family news until Asia looked up to see the giant with the radio scowling in the doorway, glaring at Paris who seemed aware but unconcerned about his presence. *Interesting.* Shaking his head in obvious frustration, he turned his attention to her.

"Asia, I'm Sheriff Trinity Stone. I'd like to ask you a few questions about what happened earlier this morning." She nodded, following him into what appeared to be an office. After she relayed her version of the events, he pointed to a screen she hadn't noticed, indicating she should watch the video he'd started. "This is a compilation of various video feeds. Tell me what you see."

None of the clips were long... hell, the entire incident had lasted less than thirty seconds, but she didn't have any trouble figuring out the bullet that grazed Franklin had been intended for her.

"How did he know?"

"He said the look on London's face was all the warning he needed." She sensed there was more to the story than he'd given her, so with well-practiced patience, she leaned back against an antique library table, crossed her arms under her ample breasts, and waited. He watched her for long seconds before sighing. "Damned lawyers are all alike." She'd have taken offense at his words if she hadn't seen the grin curving at the corners of his mouth.

"Mr. Cordesi has been working with us. He approached me after his failed attempt to scare London into coming to him for protection—an incredibly stupid move from a man who appears to otherwise be remarkably credible." Asia had already figured out he was responsible for the attack on London, but she'd also suspected his motive. Another example of someone making an incredibly bad call for the right reasons.

"We had people in place this morning—a lot of people, so we were ready. We have the shooter in custody, and he's giving up anybody and everybody. His taped confession is being forwarded to all the appropriate agencies, and he'll be in Federal custody within the hour." She straightened, standing to her full height, waiting on the words she hoped would mean she and her sisters would be safe. Nodding at her unspoken question, he continued, "Arrest warrants are already being issued for several key members of a group known as the Consortium. We won't take them all down, but the rest will back away from London—at least for a while."

"Until she's called to Washington to testify?" He nodded, confirming London would likely face more security issues in the future.

"We'll cross that bridge when we get to it." The Sheriff's words were spoken with a steely confidence Asia appreciated. Holding out her hand, she was shocked to see Trin's huge hand enclose around hers. The man's height and physical presence were almost overwhelming, yet her petite, youngest sister seemed completely unaffected. Hell, she'd deliberately ignored him in the kitchen, despite the fact he'd been studying her as if she were prey to his predator.

"Don't let him bully you, Asia. He's bossy as hell and drives like he's eighty." She hadn't heard Paris enter the room but wasn't surprised to see her sauntering across the hardwood floor, ridiculously high heels clicking with every step.

"Why didn't you stay at Evan's like you were told to? Do you ever follow rules or protocol, Paris?" The tension she'd noted in the kitchen exploded around them so thick, Asia thought about leaving, but she was afraid of missing something interesting.

"Rules? Rarely. Protocol? When it suits me."

What? Since when did her kid sister know anything about protocol? *Oh, baby girl, we are having a chat... and we're having it soon.*

Before they left the office, Asia turned to the Sheriff and asked, "Why did you show me the videos?"

"I think you already know the answer to that question, Asia. Franklin Cordesi put himself between you and a bullet this morning. If you calculate the trajectory, you'll find it would have struck you dead-center, taking out your spinal cord and heart. You'd have been gone before you hit the ground."

Trinity Stone wanted her to know she owed her life to Franklin. As much as she hated what happened to London, she was grateful London seemed to have found love. And despite her own battered ego, Asia was going to have a hard time maintaining any real animosity after what Franklin had done this morning.

Fucking hell, it chafes my ass when people are hard to hate.

Epilogue

Four months later

L ONDON LOOKED DOWN at the white dress she wore and smiled. It was remarkable what Eli and Evan had managed in such a short time. They'd offered her the wedding of her dreams, and she'd surprised them with her simple request. Lifting the front of her dress a few inches, she wiggled her bare toes in the sand and giggled.

"That's the sweetest sound in the world, baby." Evan's arms came around her, tightening below her swollen breasts until they nearly spilled over the low-cut lace.

"You are a vision, Princess. I've watched you all evening, moving through the guests, making sure everyone was having a good time. For a self-described lab-rat, you've become an amazing hostess."

Eli's words sent a rush of heat to her cheeks. Grateful for the dim lighting, she hoped they wouldn't notice how she'd flushed at the compliment. They often reminded her that it was important to accept compliments with grace, but London sometimes wondered if she would ever be completely comfortable in her new role as their mate.

She'd been pleasantly surprised by how much she enjoyed the slower work pace she'd been forced to adopt. Even though her lab was close, the changes in her body sometimes drained her of energy long before she would have ordinarily considered calling it a day.

Evan's hands smoothed over her barely noticeable bump, making her smile at his tender touch. "Your siblings were all thrilled to learn they're going to be aunts and uncles."

"It's a good thing you have plenty of guest rooms. We may have a lot of company for a while." London's heart almost burst when she walked out onto the sand to find all nine of her brothers and sisters standing along the make-shift aisle. Her walk to the driftwood altar set up where the water lapped at the shore had taken a long time, but Eli and Evan assured her seeing her happiness at their hugs and happy tears made the wait all the sweeter.

"They are always welcome. We're happy to see you building stronger bonds with your family." Their pack had welcomed her with open arms. The only reluctance she'd sensed was from a woman she'd later learned was Carolee Johnson's best friend. The nurse who'd warned London away from Evan had been questioned about her connection to the Consortium, but no charges had been filed. London didn't know where the woman was now and didn't care.

"How are you holding up, baby? We don't want you to overdo it—we have plans for you later." She couldn't hold back her giggle.

"You could have told me birth control wasn't going to be effective, you know." They'd had this conversation a dozen times, and they never showed any remorse.

"We could have, but we were distracted."

Distracted my ass, you were determined to knock me up as soon as possible. A stinging swat seared her right ass cheek making her keenly aware of the fact she was bare beneath the thin fabric of her dress.

"You are not *knocked up*. You are carrying our child. Mind your manners, mate." Evan was usually the more easygoing of her husbands, but he refused to let her refer to her pregnancy in anything but the most respectful terms.

"I hate to leave our guests, and I'm enjoying the fireworks." Trinity Stone had taken time off to attend their Caribbean wedding, and the simmering chemistry between the Sheriff and Paris was practically soap opera worthy entertainment. Paris had visited twice since the shooting and gotten speeding tickets during both trips. London knew her sister was deliberately provoking the Sheriff and had laughed out loud when she learned Trinity had threatened to paddle her bare ass the next time. Asia stood in the shadows at the edge of the large patio, talking quietly with Franklin, and London wondered if her sister had finally found a man she couldn't walk away from.

"Are you referring to Catalina and Cooper or Trinity and Paris? Seems both couples are a hot minute from spontaneously combusting." Eli's amusement was easy to hear in his voice.

"And don't overlook the very strange dynamic between Austin and Charlotte. I'm having a little trouble believing he brought her to a family wedding if she is nothing more than his assistant. I snooped and found out they're sharing a suite." Granted the suite had two bedrooms, but London still wasn't buying big brother's story.

Letting her mates lead her back to say their goodbyes, London couldn't help but wonder what the future held for the nine men and women she loved with all her heart. Building a new life with her own family didn't mean her brothers and sisters would be set aside—she intended to keep them all as close to her heart as she could. She'd had enough isolation to last a lifetime, that part of her life was in the past.

Love heals from the inside out, sweetheart.

This time her mother's whispered words brought her comfort. London had learned to accept the wisdom her mother imparted from the other side rather than being frightened by the sudden intrusions into her mind. It hadn't been easy, but Dad Jack had been a huge help, and she was forever grateful for his guidance.

London grinned at the vision dancing in her mind. Her siblings were all destined to find love, and she felt her heart swell at the realization, but knowing their paths weren't all going to be smooth sailing brought her protective instincts to the surface.

"You're going to be a wonderful mother, Princess. I can hardly wait to see your tummy round with our child."

Yeah, we'll see how you feel when I can't tie my own damned shoes.

"That's ten, Princess."

The End

Books by Avery Gale

The Adlers
Brooklyn

The ShadowDance Club
Katarina's Return – Book One
Jenna's Submission – Book Two
Rissa's Recovery – Book Three
Trace & Tori – Book Four
Reborn as Bree – Book Five
Red Clouds Dancing – Book Six
Perfect Picture – Book Seven

Club Isola
Capturing Callie – Book One
Healing Holly – Book Two
Claiming Abby – Book Three

Masters of the Prairie Winds Club
Out of the Storm
Saving Grace
Jen's Journey
Bound Treasure
Punishing for Pleasure
Accidental Trifecta
Missionary Position
Another Second Chance
Star-Crossed Miracles
Dusted Star
Lilly's Choice

The Wolf Pack Series
Mated – Book One
Fated Magic – Book Two
Tempted by Darkness – Book Three

The Knights of the Boardroom
Book One
Book Two
Book Three

The Morgan Brothers of Montana
Coral Hearts – Book One
Dancing with Deception – Book Two
Caged Songbird – Book Three
Game On – Book Four
Well Bred – Book Five

Mountain Mastery
Well Written
Savannah's Sentinel
Sheltering Reagan

The Christmas Painting
Taking Out the Mother of the Bride

I would love to hear from you!

Email: avery.gale@ymail.com

Website: www.averygale.com

Facebook: facebook.com/avery.gale.3

Twitter: @avery_gale

www.ingramcontent.com/pod-product-compliance
Lightning Source LLC
Chambersburg PA
CBHW070914180626
46817CB00003B/1056